BATTLE ROYALE
LAST FAN STANDING

Andrews McMeel Publishing
a division of Andrews McMeel Universal
1130 Walnut Street, Kansas City, Missouri 64106

www.andrewsmcmeel.com

19 20 21 22 23 RR4 10 9 8 7 6 5 4 3 2 1

ISBN: 978-1-5248-5150-7

Library of Congress Control Number: 2019934410

Made by:
LSC Communications US, LLC
Address and location of manufacturer:
2347 Kratzer Road
Harrisonburg, VA 22802
1st Printing—4/19/19

ATTENTION: SCHOOLS AND BUSINESSES
Andrews McMeel books are available at quantity discounts with bulk purchase for educational, business, or sales promotional use. For information, please e-mail the Andrews McMeel Publishing Special Sales Department: specialsales@amuniversal.com.

BATTLE ROYALE
LAST FAN STANDING

An Unofficial Fortnite Adventure

Mathias Lavorel

Andrews McMeel
PUBLISHING®

CONTENTS

1

COLD SHOWER

No . . . no . . . no . . . noooooo . . . Aaaaah . . .

No way! This is impossible . . . No, not right now . . . It's too soon!

I'm Paul. In less than one year, I'm supposed to turn eighteen. But, instead, I'm about to die.

I'm free-falling, like a rock pushed off a cliff. Every second that passes, I get closer to the hard earth below. It won't be long before I hit the ground and splat into a million pieces.

Gulp . . .

A bug or something just got stuck in my throat. Great! For the rest of my fall, no one will hear my screams anymore.

My eyes are burning, and the wind is trying to rip through my body as I somersault, head over heels, like I just found a spider in my underwear. If only I could go back in time to make the most of my last moment.

Urghhh . . . Aaaah . . . Umpph . . . Aaaah . . .

With one last effort, I manage to position myself like an airplane. Unfortunately, that doesn't mean I'm actually flying. At least I look more like a secret agent in a James Bond movie than my little sister's blankie after she's chewed on it during a two-hour car ride.

Dying so soon is awful; I won't even get to visit the big island stretching out before me. It's so beautiful with color scattered everywhere, including a lake and a desert. I can see towns, buildings, farms, a soccer field, and even swimming pools. And I love sports . . .

What's even worse is that, just a few hours ago, I landed my first acting role ever. A walk-on part, true, but it was in a blockbuster! I was going to make a name for myself, I just knew it. Now, this rising movie star is plunging toward his death at top speed. A career is falling flat before even getting started.

It's hard to imagine, but during a free-fall, the ground closes in really fast. The landscape becomes more detailed, kind of like zooming in on a picture on my phone. I think about doing a countdown, but change my mind, deciding that would be too morbid. What if I could aim for a big tree, a lake, or the sea —could I possibly survive? Aaah, it's all happening too fast! I'm doomed!

Ten minutes before

I really don't trust this bus. But in a few minutes, I'll finally be on a movie set, and I'd do anything to get there! I don't know what engineer designed this mechanical nightmare, but there

is one thing for sure: he was absolutely insane. He attached a turbine with a balloon to an old bus to make it fly. Hey, guys, when are you going to realize that not every childhood dream is meant to be brought to life? To hide the creaking of the metal, all the driver could come up with was to play music at full blast. That way, when this contraption crashes, not only will we be dead, but we will all be deaf, too. Great! I'm being negative, but we all have our own way of dealing with problems. Personally, when I have to face my fears, I like to think things through. There are about one hundred people with me, each stranger than the next. It's a miracle that we all fit in here. For now, I'm going with the flow, but I really hope someone shows up soon to tell me what to do.

All of a sudden, everyone gets up and heads toward the back of the bus, then jumps out into the open in groups of ten or fifteen. My stomach does backflips; I start shaking all over. What in the world are they doing? I press my face to a window to watch them tumble downward. OK, they must be stuntmen who are practicing. I'm sure this is normal when filming a blockbuster. Honestly, they gave me a backpack when I arrived, but I never thought it had anything to do with parachuting out of the sky! Now, I'm one of the last people onboard, and this doesn't look good. I'm starting to regret not reading the fine print in all the contracts they had me sign . . . Oops!

Hang on, just a little bit longer.

A guy near the exit waves me over to him. He's not very friendly looking. In fact, he barely manages to smile at me. As I walk over to him, I think about the last time I ate ice cream.

An acting trick to make me seem calm and relaxed. Once I'm within his reach, he lifts me up by the collar, like a mother lion carrying her cub, and, *wham*, he tosses me out into the open without a word. I look up at the sky and start screaming.

"WOULD IT HAVE KILLED YOU TO SAY GOODBYE?!?"

But actually . . . no. Not a single word comes out of my mouth. But it's not because I didn't open my mouth wide enough.

So, here I am, hurling through the open sky.

Crunch . . . Whoosh . . . Zip

I don't really understand how, but the backpack they gave me before leaving opens with a thunderous sound and turns into a sort of glider! I want to yell at the top of my lungs or laugh like a crazy person. I'M FLYING! I have no idea who decided to save me, but it looks like today is my lucky day! Drumroll, please; the rising star is back!

Splashhhhhhhh

It's freezing cold! I landed . . . well, more like belly flopped down . . . into a pond about as deep as the shallow end of a swimming pool. Before that, I had forgotten that gravity was still doing its job and I'd let go of all my troubles. I look down at my pants. I touch my legs, arms and shoulders, head . . . I feel the pressure of my hands on my body, but no pain. It looks like I'm ALIVE! And soaking wet. But alive, after all.

Wading over to the shore is hard and takes longer than I expected. I've barely set foot on the ground, and the surface of the pond is already as smooth as glass. With a quick glance, I realize my clothes are already dry. That's weird . . . But I can't tell if it's really hot or really cold. Maybe I wasn't that wet after all, and I made a big deal out of it in my head. To top it all off, whatever I was using as a parachute has disappeared. Don't panic; there has to be a logical explanation. My backpack is as light as a feather, so the material must have landed somewhere not far away, at the bottom of the pond. OK. Everything is fine. I'm still in shock. I'm starting to worry for no reason. I just need to stay calm and everything will be OK.

CALM DOWN! I'm in shock. Yes, that's it, I'm overthinking. I can't help it. That's all over, in the past. I take a moment to slowly breathe in and out to release my stress. Breeeeeeeeathe in slooooooowly through the nooooooooose . . . Hummmmmm . . . Out through the mouth . . . Whooosh!

It's something I learned from a YouTube video. After doing this three or four times, I already feel a bit better. Not being able to talk isn't a big deal; I can just act things out. With one last exhale, my shoulders and muscles relax.

What do I see here? Behind me, there's a farm with several barns. I won't go that way: I don't really like the country. More accurately, it doesn't like me. Between the poison ivy, wasps, thorny bushes, and everything in nature that makes you sick for the rest of your life, the message is clear: "Stay inside if you don't want any problems!" Which works out because that's where I'm happiest. I'm not opposed to a short outing, unless the local guide shows up in rubber boots carrying a pitchfork. A cowboy hat and piece of straw sticking out his mouth, that's fine. But, with a guard dog lunging at everyone who walks by, no thank you. So, I'll save the farm until later. If I remember correctly, during my free-fall, I saw a gas station close by. I would rather press my luck with gasoline fumes. Maybe the people there will be more inclined to help me. Besides, I'll be able to buy some candy, chocolate, or a nice treat. After that fall, I deserve it.

There must be a film crew somewhere, and I'm gonna find them. A blockbuster about superheros with villains from outer space bent on taking over the world; it's going to be a big hit! I absolutely have to be in this film. That's what I signed up for, after all! With all those papers they had me sign, one thing is for sure: they have my name, and they know I'm coming! They must already be looking for me. First, I have to climb to the top of this hill in front of me, and then I'll decide what to do next. By getting a little higher up, I'll have a better view so I can get my bearings.

Strangely, I feel great. I'm bouncing around like a little kid. Hop, hop, hop, I jump here and there while I make my way up the side of the hill. OK, I admit that wasn't the longest climb ever, but I don't feel tired at all. It must be the excitement . . . Even though I don't like the country, it feels good to be outside.

I reach the top and see several trees. The area seems to have lots of rolling hills. In the other direction, below and to the right, I think I see the gas station, but in front of me, a little farther away, there are some really strange structures. They look like pagodas, like at the

Asian restaurant where I love to eat. There's something strange about buildings like that being in the middle of the country. Hmmm. Those buildings must be part of the movie set! This future movie star didn't leave his brain at home, and that's good news. Forget the gas station; next stop, Little China!

I have to hike down one hill, then climb another. This is good for my health! I hadn't noticed it earlier, but now a tiny temple perched on a hill top catches my attention. A curious light is shining inside. I'm dying to stop by, but that wouldn't make sense. I can't lose focus; my goal is to get to that restaurant-looking building. It's a tower with several stories. I think there will be more people over there, and at least I won't be running the risk of offending a god who will curse my family for forty generations. I follow a winding path, and as I get closer, I'm less convinced that it's occupied. I see picnic tables, which gives the place a very homey feel.

Suddenly, I hear footsteps. Someone is running inside. A door slams, and, if I'm right, he or she must be rushing down the stairs. I try to shout to make my presence known, but there's still no sound coming out of my mouth. Jeez! I have no idea what happened to me when I fell, but I'm going to have to use my awesome acting skills to show who I am and what I want. Urgghh . . . With my great luck so far, I'm going to end up in an ambulance wearing a straitjacket.

While I was thinking, the sounds stopped. I continue to approach, and suddenly I hear a buzzing sound.

Crrrrrrrrraacck! Boooooom!

A bizarre explosion. Was that person hurt? I'd better hurry up, because, if so, everything could change in just a few seconds. I run to the door like a madman, yank it open, and hurry into the room. No one's home. There are columns and wooden stairs, but not a single piece of furniture. Then, I hear a strange whistle. Something hits me and I feel really tired all of a sudden. I look behind me where the door is still wide open, and I think I see someone. Another whistle and everything gets blurry. Without warning, I lose consciousness.

2

HERE WE GO AGAIN

I slowly open my eyes. I feel perfect! I'm standing next to a landing strip. All around me, people are dancing, playing with fake guns, or just standing around like me. Out on the tarmac, partly disassembled, is a humongous bus, tricked out like it should be in a movie. We're waiting for them to fix it and take us to a film shooting location. Despite all of the warnings—well, teasing actually—I landed a role in a blockbuster. Hollywood and I are made for each other, and I'm going to prove it to the world.

I feel really bizarre; this wait's taking forever. Plus, I have the strange feeling I've experienced this before. They say déjà-vu is the brain's response to a stressful situation. But something feels odd, like I just had a dream about this. I must have dozed off . . . Usually, I don't remember my dreams, but now everything comes rushing back to me: falling through the sky, the deserted Asian house, the explosion . . .

I nervously check myself for any injuries. Nothing. No pain or even muscle cramps . Everything seems normal . . .

"THE COMBAT BUS LEAVES IN TEN SECONDS!"

Oh jeez! What's this thing? Could the mechanics have fixed up that beat-up bus so fast? I swallow with some difficulty. In my dream, this machine was flying, but that seems impossible now . . . There must be a giant elevator under the bus. It's just Hollywood magic, where things aren't always as they seem. I'd be crazy to miss my opportunity. I have to climb on the bus to get to the film shoot—especially since I have no idea where that is. All these confidentiality procedures are ridiculous.

I sit down on a very uncomfortable seat. My throat gets tight. Everything is happening like it did in my dream . . . Breathe. I scoot over to the window. I always go for the window seat, that way I can look outside and avoid the other passengers. Especially when my neighbor smells like stinky feet! I just have to glue myself to the window and everything will be fine! Except that one time when the glass was especially dirty and I got someone else's boogers on my nose. I sure looked silly . . . Ohhh! No, no, no! After a few seconds, the machine takes off. I look around to see the others' reactions. A FLYING BUS! Everyone seems to think it's normal. I guess I'll play it cool, too. I don't want to look like a wimp.

This is wild—we're already pretty high up in the air. The bus is heading toward a big island. As we move in that direction, I see that our starting point was on an island, too, but a much smaller one. These two strips of land don't seem very far apart. I wonder why we're not taking a boat, or at least some other vehicle that complies with safety codes. Maybe this is part of the film.

Uh oh. They opened the back doors and everyone is getting ready to leave. It must be . . . uhhh . . . duh . . . Gulp. OK, this is not looking good. Everything is happening just like it did in my dream!

Now, let's see if there's an easier way off the bus . . . I'm the last one again, and a guy who looks like he belongs in the military waves me over. To keep my nightmare from happening again, I try to walk over very slowly. I stand up, move calmly toward him, and hit my chest two times with my fist to show him that I'm a cool guy. We're bros; I don't want any trouble. As I get within his reach, I start explaining to him . . .

. . .

What the heck?! I'm mute. My teachers and family would be extremely happy to know I'm being quiet for once. But I wish I could . . .

Aaahhhhh . . .

The big brute is all action and no talk. He throws me out the door as if I were a bag of potatoes! I don't know his name, I don't know anything about him, but I HATE him! I finally realize I didn't imagine it. This whole thing has happened before . . . It's awful! The sky, the speed, the sound, and the earth getting closer every second! I'm terrified! Breathe. You know what to do . . . First, get in the right position . . .

Grrrr . . . Hurrruuumph . . .

TA-DA! I'm facing downward, arms and legs spread out to slow my fall. Then, I start fiddling with my pack to open . . .

CRUNCH . . . WHOOSH . . . ZIP

. . . my guardian angel. Oh, God! Everything about this glider is unnatural. It's practically falling apart! It makes a horrible sound and feels like it's about to break apart into campfire wood at any second . . . This is crazy. What did I do to deserve this? I can't come up with any rational reason why this is happening . . . I feel like I'm about to cry, and I never cry.

I arrive above what looks like a factory, and my trajectory leads me to the middle of a field that clearly functions as a parking lot. In the distance, I think I see the Asian temple from the last time. In a few seconds, I'll be on the ground. This time, there's no water, instead it's actual earth. Uh-oh. I close my eyes and focus the best I can, like I'm a Jedi Master using the force.

Plop . . .

Wow! Not bad! Not exactly the most elegant landing, but at least I've still got all my limbs. I stand up straight, feeling pretty good. I can breathe a sigh of relief. This place is deserted. I'd love to see another human, a normal person who wants to talk about the weather, sports, or anything at all. In the middle of the nearby field, perched on a massive column, is the biggest building I've ever seen. There's no doubt about it; the universe is sending me a very clear message. If I had my phone, I would post this on Instagram and get a million comments.

Nothing makes sense. I suddenly start looking closely at everything around me. Is there a hidden camera somewhere? Maybe this is some kind of a test to see if I have the skills to be the next action movie star! I look up at the sky and point toward the clouds. No sound comes out of my mouth, but the message in my eyes is saying, "Hey! You up there! You don't know who I'm yet, but you will soon. I'm THE star who's going to make it all the way to the top. Oh, yes."

That little inner rant felt good. At any rate, it's not like I had a choice, and staying here feeling sorry for myself wouldn't change a thing. As long as I'm here, I might as well try to find some help inside the factory. At that exact moment, I hear the same sound I heard at the temple. A strange buzzing. This time it sounds like it's coming from a dump truck parked close by. By the way, I love those trucks. I had one when I was little. It could carry everything: my stuffed animal, my old 3DS, even my little sister.

What's weird is that there's a bright light coming out of the dumpster. I would need to climb inside to find the source, but at the same time, I'm afraid someone will catch me snooping. What a terrible first impression that would make! I'd better not.

The closer I get to the building, the clearer it becomes that the place is completely deserted, just like before. How crazy! What's happening on this island? Still lost in my own thoughts, I jump when I see someone appear out of thin air on the factory roof. She's wearing a pink bear costume, her automatic rifle pointed directly at my head. I don't move, frozen in shock. You don't see that every day. A teddy bear, armed to the teeth, with guns aimed right at me. There's not enough time to find out if it's one of those toys laying around at the bus airport, is it . . .

BRrrrrraAAAaaa BRrrraaaAAAA BrrrrrAAAaaaaa . . .

I slowly open my eyes. I feel fine. I look around me, and . . . NO WAY!! I'm back at the landing strip. Not again! What's going on?? Not only did I faint again, but I'm back on the small island.

In a moment of panic, I run up to the people around me, one by one, hoping to see someone with an understanding gaze, hoping to find some reassurance. It's worse than ever. In return, I only get danced at, shot at, or totally ignored. With one last effort, I put my drama classes to use. I do everything that I can think of to imitate being in a mental prison: walking in circles, then backward, and crouching down. No success. I burst into tears.

Bawling, my head in my hands, I sense a presence. Slowly peeking between my fingers, I see a pair of shoes a few inches away from mine. I pull myself together and try to put on a brave face. A boy about my age is standing there, almost touching me, not moving. Instinctively, I take a step back. Then, and nothing could have prepared me for this, he executes a series of frenzied dance moves—dabs. That's it. I'm in the middle of a living nightmare. There's no other tangible explanation for all this. No one would do that in real life—no one. My mind must be playing tricks on me. This has to be some kind of stress-induced hallucination. Like on the first day of school, imagine I'm on the

playground missing a shoe, even my pants. This must be the same kind of thing, because of stress. I'll wake up RIGHT NOW!

"THE COMBAT BUS LEAVES IN TEN SECONDS!"

Nothing is happening like it's supposed to. I'm going crazy. I jump into the vehicle without thinking. No more Mr. Nice Guy. You want to play this game? Let's play! The bus starts dropping off nut jobs, as usual. Once the first half have jumped, I gather my courage and, with about ten other people, I jump out into the open.

YEAHHHHHHHHHH

Clearly, I'm acting like everything is fine, even though I don't know what's happening. All around me, I notice that some people open their glider right away. How'd they do that? I start running my hands over my chest and . . .

CRUNCH . . . WHOOSH . . . ZIP

. . . Oh, wow, it worked! There's a button somewhere that opens this thing! Aaahhhhh!

CRUNCH . . . WHOOSH . . . ZIP

Noooo! I don't know what I did, but the whole thing just closed up and I'm falling at top speed again, zig-zagging between the soldiers.

CRUNCH . . . WHOOSH . . . ZIP . . . AAAhhhh . . .

Near the ground, the crazy ride finally stops, and my glider stays open and stabilizes. Phew. I'm above a big town. There are buildings, a basketball court, and . . . I don't have time to take it all in before I hear whistling all around me. Underneath me is an anthill of sharpshooters firing at anything that moves. What on earth is happening on this island? Is this part of the blockbuster? Are they filming without telling us? On the sets I've seen (just on TV), there were lights, cameras, and technicians. But here, I don't see any signs of that.

One on my right, one on my left, and two above me. The bullets start flying at me. When I lean forward to try to dodge them, I realize that it's changing the trajectory of my descent. OK, so there has to be a way to steer this thing. Ow! I think I'm hit. I start feeling tired like the other times before I passed out. Hurry . . . turn, adjust, swerve. The shooting becomes more hectic, and I do everything I can to get away from the danger zone. I twirl around to dodge the bullets as gracefully as a plastic bag caught in the wind. I'm about to land several feet from a garage with a half-open door. I'll have to crawl underneath it. I'm trying to reach it when, once again, night falls and . . . curtain.

I slowly open my eyes. I feel perfect! NO! I'm back on the small island and nothing has changed. Everyone is acting like before, like this is normal! Why the heck are they firing tranquilizers at people, without saying anything? Hey, guys! My vaccinations are up-to-date, no need to put me under. Plus, I got all my boosters before coming here, so isn't it time to change targets? And if you think you're going to tame the wild beast sleeping inside of me, *SPOILER ALERT,* you're doing exactly the opposite!

Five times, ten times, thirty times, I've climbed in this awful bus. No matter where I land, whether I run or walk, I keep getting shot down, riddled with bullets, impaled on hidden spikes in walls, and even blown to bits with rocket launchers. Whether I fall into the sea, or jump from a bridge or from a mountain, the outcome never changes. No matter the location and length of my excursions, it's always the same story. Right back to the small island. Don't pass Go. Don't collect two hundred dollars. I have to figure this out; I'm locked in this prison! This means that what's true for me is also true for the others. If only I could talk! I'm going crazy . . . I need to talk to someone.

3

WHICH WAY TO THE EXIT?
(SMALL ISLAND)

I don't sleep. I don't dream. I'm officially being held captive on two islands that I'll now call. Small Island and Big Island. It makes me feel a little better to name things and people I don't know well, or at all.

What day is it? How long have I been here? A week? Two? With all this chaos, I haven't even counted how many days and nights have passed. Let's think. There are always two sides to every coin: if I got into this, I can get out of it. I just need a plan and some discipline. I'll start my search here, on Small Island. That's how I got here, surely that's where I'll have the most luck finding an exit.

It seems this place has very strict rules, and they aren't written down anywhere. Some apply to both islands, but each has its own unique characteristics. Here's what I've learned so far: I can't talk. I don't know how, but my vocal cords are obstructed. The days go by and I don't need to eat, drink, or sleep. So there's no waiting in line at the bathroom. Why dedicate a factory to them then? It must be because all the buildings are just movie sets. That would explain why all the sites are empty and deserted. Could it be temporary? If I investigate, I'll eventually get to the bottom of it.

"THE COMBAT BUS LEAVES IN TEN SECONDS!"

In my window seat, I think long and hard. Anything that gets destroyed reappears every time, in the same place. Small Island is the starting point. Anything goes here without any consequences for anyone. This is where we regain consciousness, and fainting here is absolutely impossible. But when the bus is ready to take off, everyone has to get onboard, without any exceptions. That forces me to go back and forth constantly between the two islands. I've tried every way of cheating, but the tough guy on the bus always finds me and grabs me. He also always throws me out if I refuse to jump.

As for Big Island, all I know so far is that we quickly lose consciousness there. Why do we have to go there? What's over there? Why are all those people fighting? So many questions that are still unanswered. I'll tackle that island and its problems later. First, I'll focus on Small Island. It won't take me long to see the whole thing, and hopefully I can find something to help me. In the meantime, I leap out into the open.

Now, I've come to like opening my glider right after jumping. I can't believe I'm saying that, but it's true. Soaring at that altitude is one of the only times when I feel almost peaceful. The wind carrying me, the beautiful island below me, and the slow descent when I can go wherever I want; it all gives me a sense of freedom that means more and more to me. During these moments, I find the energy to keep going.

I slowly arrive above the largest city. In a few seconds, I'll be under fire. I've discovered that landing in such a popular place is the most effective way to faint. That's it; I hear the first explosions. It won't be long before I lose consciousness. Cool, I can't wait to start exploring Small Island!

I slowly open my eyes to see the usual hustle and bustle at the landing strip.

It's time for the grand tour. Due to the bus's constant departures, I'll need more than ten round trips to get an accurate picture of Small Island. Not much vegetation, trees scattered everywhere, some uninteresting hills. There is an abandoned airfield with discarded cars on it, a few random buildings and hangars, and a shipping area with empty containers. The army must have used it before. You can tell by the wooden training course and obstacle course made of tires.

I love tires! The exercise consists of finishing the course without falling on your butt. You have to run across it, being careful to step in the center of each tire, where the rim would normally go. Like a trampoline, the fun part is being able to bounce up when you jump on a tire! Who knows what purpose it serves, but it's really fun.

It feels good to laugh a little, because this place has been stressing me out. It seems like life disappeared in a split second, like a curse took it away. But I can't think about that. As for the access routes, reaching the sea on foot is impossible. Not only is there no path leading to it, but some kind of unusually powerful magnetic field also keeps everything from getting too close to the cliffs overlooking it. I also looked for a tunnel entrance—but again, no success. No trapdoor in sight, even though I carefully inspected every building. I also took the time to search the bushes and other vegetation, hoping I might find an underground entrance.

Only the airways are left to explore. That's where things get interesting. In addition to the landing strip used by the bus, there is a helicopter landing pad. So far, I haven't seen or heard anything arrive. Who knows though? I'll keep my eyes and ears open.

At first glance, my assessment seems pretty grim, but this research has taught me all kinds of things about the people here. First, the ratio of boys to girls is pretty even. Quite a few of them wear masks and helmets, making it hard to identify them. Also, I don't know where they got them. Do they have a use? A purpose? I can see that I still have a lot to discover here . . .

Anyway, there are five big groups of people. Obviously, that's an average because there are always exceptions and special cases:

✱ THE TRIGGER-HAPPY PSYCHOPATHS: Small Island is filled with fake guns. Just bend over and pick one up. These objects are noisy and harmless to people, but they destroy the environment. These people empty magazine after magazine, even though it doesn't do anything. It's their way of killing time (great!).

* **THE CLEARERS**: They're like the trigger-happy psychopaths, but more effective. They work with tangible materials. They like to wipe everything out, producing a clearly visible result. They want to clear everything, get rid of it all. They're the environment's worst nightmare. If I ever want to do some home remodeling, I'll turn to one of them.

* **THE BUILDERS**: They're the opposite of the clearers. They use every second they have to build structures. They work with wood, stone, and metal. Very fast and very effective, they like to gather and recycle raw materials to invest in new things. Their guilty pleasure is scaling the structures they build as fast as possible. If they could open their arms and shout "I'm the king of the world!" from the top of their structure, they would do it every time! The builder's worst enemy is the clearer. As soon as a single wall appears, war breaks out. Both groups are extremely stubborn, resulting in surreal scenes in which the one group rebuilds nonstop in the same spot, while the others do their best to destroy it (perfect!).

* **THE PARTIERS**: At first glance, they're the most fun. They strike funny poses, dance, and do graffiti. But look a little closer, and you'll see they're the scariest. When you think about the context, you wonder what could be so thrilling to a normal person, especially when that person is stuck

in prison and can't say a word! Who would do that? Crazy people.

And, speaking of crazy people, the last category is just about as bad:

* **THE STANDSTILLS**: They don't move an inch. They're real statues. It's kind of like having a pet rock. They have no interaction with the rest of the world. To the point that trying to move one has become a sort of game to the "residents." It's impossible. You can pull on them, build on them, paint them, but nothing affects them. It's like they're completely resigned to their lot in life. It's fascinating and frightening at the same time.

I've noticed that certain standstills believe in rituals. They don't just stand around randomly. Most go back to the exact same places over and over again.

I noticed it the second or third time I ran past the helicopter pad. She was standing up straight, not arrogantly, but with her feet planted firmly on the ground, with her shoulders back. She didn't exactly stand out either. I wondered how long she had been there before I noticed her. I stopped short to watch her. Clearly, she did not move. She was right in the middle of the circle, her feet placed perfectly on the horizontal line of the H painted on the tarmac. I couldn't imagine that this very unusual position was just a happy accident. So, I kept exploring, keeping that in mind. I was reminded of the walking sticks you see in aquariums.

The insects that look like wood and camouflage themselves. Once you see one, you start to see all the others. The same thing happened to me here. Almost all the standstills I saw were in specific locations in specific stances. Incredible.

Once again, the question is: are we all human beings? Or, are we surrounded by clones and robots? No one bleeds, sneezes, or spits. There is no liquid anywhere, and that thought scares me to death. One more reason to find the exit ASAP!

In any event, I know one thing for sure: my salvation is not here. Small Island is only a transportation platform; the exit's over there, on Big Island. I'm going to keep exploring and I'll find a way out of this mess!

"THE COMBAT BUS LEAVES IN TEN SECONDS!"

4

WHERE'S THE EXIT?
(BIG ISLAND)

From the bus window, I scan Big Island's topography. It's somewhat disk-shaped with irregular features. It looks like a messed-up pancake. Like someone dripped the batter in the pan without paying any attention to the results. In the center of the island, a large lake is easy to spot. It feeds two rivers that flow into the sea. One goes north; the other goes south. I'll use that line to guide my exploration.

To the west is a mountainous region with extremely high peaks. The largest towns are located there. The east consists of vast plains and appears to be the agricultural sector of the island. This rundown wouldn't be complete without mentioning the small desert region in the southeast. Explaining its presence is hard. Is the surface different down there? Maybe it's a micro-climate? If I had spent less time drawing on my desk during geography, I might understand it better . . .

Where should I start? My priority is to avoid losing consciousness as much as possible. The less I faint, the more time I'll have on the ground, and the more effective I'll be. So I have to become invisible and blend into my environment. I have to become a chameleon, a role made just for me. The bus route is very simple, a straight line from one end of the island to the other. The "residents" throw themselves out of the bus as soon as possible, so I'll jump at the last minute every time. Once I'm outside, I'll aim for an isolated spot along the coast. I'm sure no one will arrive by sea, so that limits the chances of someone sneaking up from behind to surprise me. If I see any potential threats in the distance, I'll have time to figure out a solution.

Everyone else has already jumped out. I surprise the tough guy on the bus when I leave my seat. I look him in the eyes and give him a knowing look. Don't waste your energy, buddy; I know my way out. "Hasta la vista, baby!" I know he didn't hear me, but I like to think he did. I leap out into the open.

I dive head-first toward my fate. Even though the odds of being shot down in the air are almost zero, I would rather not stay there for too long. The hunt is on, and target shooting is one of the most popular games here.

CRUNCH . . . WHOOSH . . . ZIP

The day is almost over. In the distance, I can see the sun quickly setting behind the island. The light casts a golden sheen over the landscape. Caught up in its beauty, I forget who I am and why I'm here for a brief second. It's amazing. I would love to share this moment with someone. Not necessarily holding that person's hand or looking into her eyes but just to have her next to me, enjoying the same thing as me. I'm a fool! I just need to post an Instagram story! Next thing I know, I'm overcome with heartache, sharp and intense. This is no time for "sharing your life." Instead it's "escape if you can."

By the time I return to reality, my feet land on the grass. Behind me is a cliff and the sea below it. In front of me are two large trees hiding a small wooden cabin. Perfect! What a great starting point! I hurry over to the cabin.

I've had a little time to think. Clearly, the island's secrets don't lie on its surface, but underneath it. Except for the flying bus, I've not seen any other air traffic, and since I arrived, no boats. Since all the destroyed structures are practically replaced at the speed of light, this means there is a large storage area somewhere nearby. And where better than underground to keep tons of material out of sight? There must be enormous underground hangars connected to the surface by tunnels. I'll just have to enter one and wait for a truck, train, or some kind of vehicle making deliveries to arrive so that I can escape. Easy as pie. The first stage is clear: find a way to get down there. Even if I don't find an elevator, or whatever device they use to carry materials to the surface, there must be an air duct or emergency exit leading to this gigantic area. I may not have graduated high school yet, but my head isn't completely full of rocks either!

As with Small Island, the plan is to scour all the buildings and plants, anything that could camouflage a hatch, an air duct, or a secret door.

More motivated than ever, I hurry to get to the cabin. I've just passed the first tree, when a sound coming from inside stops me in my tracks. A muffled explosion. The last time I heard that sound, things did not turn out well for me. I have to act fast.

I'm sure someone is going to come out and happily hand me a return ticket to Small Island. Several yards away there is a bush. I run toward it like it's a childhood friend I haven't seen in ten years. I scoot underneath it and hide there, petrified and completely still. I hear fast, heavy footsteps on the stairs. But they stop suddenly. Whoever it is must have heard me.

Suddenly, I itch all over. Must be nerves. Unless it's insects like spiders, cockroaches, or ants? Maybe even a snake, right under me . . . Gulp. I have a fear of insects; I'm terrified they'll crawl into my ears, my mouth, or my nose without me realizing it. The thought scares me to death. This is my worst nightmare. I only want to do one thing: run out of here scratching myself all over. Calm down! I'm just nervous, that's all.

The footsteps start up again. I hear just a few, intermittently. He—or she—must be looking for me. I just have to get through this, then everything will be fine. Suddenly, everything speeds up. The "resident" tears around the area, consistently leaping up to perform quarter-turns and get a full view of the terrain. He goes past, only a few yards away, without seeing me. He stops, turns around, comes back toward me, then starts leaping away again and disappears behind a hill. Phew . . .

That was a close call. I thought I was going to have to go back to Small Island before exploring even a single building.

I finally leave the bush. I check myself for creepy-crawlies. But everything is fine, and the coast is clear. Two tiny butterflies flutter around me. I consider this a good omen. Mother Nature is on my side. I love that.

I hurry inside the cabin. The inside is mostly barren with only a floor, walls, ceiling . . . Oh, look! I spot one stairway to the second floor, and another to the basement! Perfect. I rush down the steps two at a time. I cannot wait to get out of this awful place . . .

"... TSSSHHH ... ARROW ... FOR ... TSSSHHH IN TSSSHHH MINUTES!"

Oh, man, they just made an announcement! Because of the static, I couldn't understand it. We all have a small radio in our backpacks that broadcasts information from time to time. But unfortunately, I don't have a clue what that alert said. That's OK! I'm sure I'll find out soon enough.

I reach the downstairs, but I'm disappointed because there is still no sign of a potential exit. It's just a basement with an electric meter, a broken-down water heater, an old sleeping bag, paper everywhere, and a suitcase. Something catches my attention though. A massive wooden chest is sitting in one corner. I get closer and see that it's empty. I think the muffled explosion was the sound of it opening. Does this mean everyone knows how to break locks?

I rifle through my backpack, looking for a lock pick or some kind of tool. The only thing I find is a map. Why didn't I think of looking at it sooner? It's a fairly accurate representation of Big Island. Right away, I begin looking for a specific symbol indicating an exit. That would be great, but I decide to finish exploring the cabin first and then I'll go back to looking at this. I go upstairs and climb up to the top floor. There's an opening onto a tiny balcony that overlooks the beautiful scenery. I don't know what idiot built this shack, but it faces the plains, even though the sea is some ten yards away on the other side. I swear, some people . . . From here, I can see a nice town below and to the left, but I'll stay away from there for now.

I sit down to examine the map. I turn it around and around, looking at it from every angle in case it contains a transparent message. Nothing. That's OK. It will still let me mark all the places I've visited so that I know what's left to explore. That will save me so much time!

Freedom awaits! I leap down to the foot of the cabin and depart in the safest direction. A winding pathway slopes uphill. The space is too open for my liking, but I have no other choice. A lamppost catches my attention, with a shelter below. The building does not seem very interesting, but sometimes big things come in small packages. I rush up to it, while keeping an eye on my surroundings. I arrive safely in front of its iron door, which has a lightning bolt symbol on it. It must be an electrical room. As my fingers slowly reach for the doorknob, I pray I won't get electrocuted. My heart beats faster, harder. I gather my courage and grab it!

"GGGGNN ••• TTTSSSHHH •••
NNIIIIIIIII ••• SECONDS!"

Oh no! The loud creak from the metal door completely muffled the announcement. Well, at least I wasn't electrocuted, so that's not so bad. I go inside, shutting the door behind me. Never mind that sound.

I feel like the entire island could have heard it. I can't stay here long. My survey of the room is quick, since there is nothing inside besides an old armchair and a beat-up metal filing cabinet. Unfortunately, there is no sign of an underground entrance. Time for that horrible creak again . . .

Even though everything inside of me is telling me to shut this door, I can't make myself do it. The sound is so awful. To escape as quickly as possible, I decide to follow the path, still heading away from the town. There are shrubs lining one side. I'll be able to hide in them to examine my map and find the best place to explore next. When I reach the first bush, I verify that it's bug-free like the last one. Incredibly, yes, it's super clean. I carefully crawl inside and unfold the map. I mark the places I've already been and trace my path. That way, if I search all the buildings without finding anything, I'll know exactly which unexplored areas are left to visit.

While I'm focused on not missing anything, I hear an announcement, very clearly this time. It's confusing, to say the least.

"YOU'RE IN THE STORM: RUN!"

5

YOU'RE IN THE STORM: RUN!

I don't feel well. I'm not sure if it's because this message made me anxious or something in the air changed, but I'm having trouble breathing. I have to get moving. In a panic, I put away my map and leave the bush. Outside, it's chaos on earth! I've never seen anything quite like this. The world is now bathed in an eerie, purple light. The sky looks like a stormy sea, interspersed with sparks of lightning bolts and deafening thunder booms. On top of it all, huge gusts of wind transform the tiny raindrops into arrows pummeling my face. The best advice I've heard comes from the radio in my backpack: "Run!"

But where to? In which direction? I'm like a deer caught in the headlights, paralyzed by fear. I glance all around me; I don't know what to do. In front of me, about a hundred yards away, is a wooden cabin, standing on top of four columns, resembling a hunting blind. That could be the solution. Either way, seeing it gives me back the use of my legs. I take off running. I get closer, but notice that there is no ladder to climb up to it. I'll have to find another way. As I run, I feel the life draining out of my body, little by little, like a faucet left running. At this rate, I won't last long. I have to find refuge fast. I run alongside a small hill. While I circle it, the horizon expands to offer me a very unexpected view. An enormous blue barrier, somewhat transparent, seems to be

containing the storm. What's this thing? Without stopping, I keep my eyes on this phenomenon stretching from the sky to the ground. I don't know if this thing is solid, electrical, dangerous, or, above all, if I'll be able to go through it! I don't have a choice, so I head straight for it. As I get closer, the details become clearer. It's covered in white stripes and made of a moving material that makes it appear alive. On the other side, the air seems really clear.

Only a few more yards to go. I slow my stride so I can push off my stronger foot and put as much power and range as possible into my jump. One, two, three! At full speed, I shoot into the air and close my eyes. I swing my arms to make my flight go as far as possible, and . . . BINGO! I land on the other side, without a scratch. Phew. That was close. Now I can breathe normally, and I feel so much better. In the time I've been here, that was the first time I've seen such a disaster. What could have set off that freak storm? Clearly, there are more surprises in store for me here.

The barrier emits a distinct rumbling sound. I'm pretty sure it's a magnetic field—or something like that—that can hold back the chaos on the other side. I can't stop myself from approaching it to take a closer look. It's as thin as a veil. Transparent squares appear and disappear randomly on its surface, like a computer going haywire. I want to touch it, just to see what happens. My heart thumps faster in my chest. I jumped through it earlier without a problem, so there's no reason this should go badly. I slowly approach it. I'm about to reach out and touch it, when I step on something soft that grosses me out. I look down to see what I just smooshed . . .

Oh! A mushroom. Not just any mushroom, but a blue one. That's kind of a big change. I crouch down and examine it. In the meantime, I hear six whizzing sounds. I'm positive what caused them is an automatic weapon. The real question is, where is that gun? I could swear the shots came from inside the storm.

So, I stick my head through the barrier to check. My mouth is barely through, when I feel myself suffocating. I have to leave, but I'm hypnotized by what I see before me. A man or woman, I can't really say, leaps over and stops right in front of me. His handgun spits out bullets as fast as the magazine loads them. The path he takes through the storm, combined with his series of leaps and bounds, makes his aim almost useless. But what fascinates me the most is that his head is a gigantic tomato! I rub both of my eyes and blink. He is only a few yards away from me when he suddenly vanishes into thin air. A small drone appeared above his head and seemed to suck him up before it disappeared, too. All that's left is a handgun and some ammo.

Stomach pains surge through me, serving as a reminder that I have to leave this contaminated area. I leap backward. What kind of crazy place have I been sent to? I take several deep breaths to try to release the pressure inside my stomach. What's going on? I look around me. Aside from the barrier's rumbling, everything is calm, as if nothing happened. I feel utterly lost again. I'm having a hard time telling the difference between real and not real. After all, isn't it possible I was just hallucinating because of the poisonous gas in the storm? How will I know? It doesn't do me any good to stand here doing nothing; I have to focus on my goal and continue exploring.

On my right side, in the distance, several evergreens loom over a group of buildings. They look like hangars to me. Closer to me, on my left side, two houses face each other. That may not be the most likely place for an underground tunnel, but nothing is as it seems here, so it may be worth taking a look around. If I don't find anything, there will be time to go inspect the hangars. Relieved that I escaped the storm, but still slightly shaken, I walk calmly toward my next destination. Oh, man! The mushroom! After all that, I almost forgot about it. I'm about to turn back when my radio starts crackling with a foreboding message:

"THE EYE OF THE STORM IS SHRINKING..."

I stop short. I barely have enough time to turn around before I'm overtaken by drizzle, gusts of wind, raindrops that feel like knives, and the purple light. The protective barrier moves away at breakneck speed. I rush after it. I run as fast as possible, but it's not enough. It's faster than me. I have one hope, though: the houses. I run toward the first one I see.

Just a few more yards before I can get inside. I pray that the door is unlocked or, at least, that someone inside is willing to let me in. I leap over a small fence (no time for manners), grab the doorknob, turn it, and . . . IT'S A MIRACLE!

The door opens with a creak. I hastily close it behind me and notice, with dismay, that this has no effect on the raging storm. Gulp. Nothing changed. Maybe it's because the windows are open? I check out the entire ground floor. I cross a tiny entryway, and find a kitchen leading directly to the bottom of a staircase. Everything appears to be shut down. I race up the stairs, two at a time, heading toward the bedrooms. I arrive on a landing where I start to have trouble breathing. Up here, everything is closed up, too. I go into a bedroom only to discover that it's the only room on this floor. There's nowhere to take shelter from this poison that's depleting my health little by little. Without a second thought, I shoot back downstairs. Perhaps the basement will be more isolated. If I'm lucky, I'll find a bathroom. At school, a fireman showed us how to shut yourself inside one in case of a fire. I remember it exactly. You get a towel wet, stuff it under the door, and hunker down in the shower stall, or even better, the bathtub if there is one. Once I reach downstairs, I find myself disappointed again.

Despite the fact that everything is shut, the storm has overtaken every nook and cranny of the building. It's raining indoors! How in the world is that possible? I can tell it won't be long before I faint. What kind of house has no bathroom?! What should have been a basement turned out to be an office. One corner contained a musty couch. I don't care about fleas or mites right now; I don't have the strength or desire to look for another solution, so I'll just lay down here for now. As I settle in the cheap cushions, I perform my deep-breathing exercise to try to calm down, but it doesn't help. With each breath, I feel a little weaker. There are shelves next to me containing servers and other computer hardware. A big, well-lit desk sits a bit farther away. Two large flight cases occupy a corner, and there's even an enormous camera on a giant, wheeled stand! I use the last of my energy to stand up and go touch it. I want to make sure it's not a hallucination. It's beautiful. It has all kinds of buttons and levers to change the settings. I've never seen one in real life. How cool! A real movie camera! That's when it hits me. Half of the room is painted neon green! I look closely at one of the walls to check. Scratching at it reveals the surface underneath. Surely this is that specific kind of paint the professionals use for special effects! My heart starts racing; I have in front of me everything needed for a professional film shoot. This is it! I've found the first solid proof that there really is a camera crew on this island!

I'm exhausted, but at least I didn't do all of this for nothing. I pull out my map to mark this spot. I don't know what this storm has in store for me, what the repercussions will be on the rest of my journey here, but if possible, I'll come back here later and check things out. My dream is to be a part of a film, and I hope to make that happen! No matter what challenges I have to overcome, or no matter how much time it takes, I'll do it. I never would have imagined it would be this difficult. But I have to keep the faith and be optimistic and positive: I've been right from the start! I know it and I always knew it. I was made to be an actor, a star . . .

6

THIRD DOOR TO THE RIGHT

Several months before . . .

"Paul!" my dad yells. "Open your eyes, young man . . . You will never be an actor. Besides, acting isn't even a real job. Instead of standing there with your mouth hanging open catching flies, go study for the SAT!"

He looks over from the TV. "What's that you have there??"

With my hand trembling with fear and excitement, I wave a newspaper page with an ad circled in yellow under my father's nose. He grabs it, adjusts his glasses, and starts to read, half-swallowing his words.

"Hmm . . . URGENT: seeking actors for a film blah, blah, blah . . . Are you serious? Do you really think this will make you someone important? What's your life plan? Do you want to end up living under a bridge?"

I grab the crumpled paper out of his hands and walk away, grumbling, back to my bedroom.

"Well, don't come crying to me or asking for anything when I become a star!"

"You'll see; you'll thank me later for saving you time!!"

Two months before . . .

I'm feverish. My hands are trembling. The envelope I'm holding seems to weigh a ton, if not more. I never get any letters in the mail. Emails, WhatsApp notifications, that kind of thing, but never letters. Nothing written on real paper. Well . . . maybe I'm exaggerating a bit: I do get ads and junkmail, but I never waste my time opening them. The important stuff always ends up in my mother's hands. But this, this is different. The address is in my handwriting, which is strange, almost like I sent it to myself. I take a deep breath and open it.

"Dear Sir, We are pleased to inform you that your application was accepted for the film to be directed by Jane Doe. Please come to . . . "

YEAHHHH!!! With a shout, I jump onto my bed and bounce up and down several times, like I'm trying to stomp out a huge fire. I kiss the letter, over and over. Always believe in yourself; always follow your dreams.

One month before . . .

I stand in front of an amazingly huge building. How many people would it take to fill this skyscraper's offices? A ton, I bet . . . I'm holding my precious letter tightly in my hands. I glance back and forth between the paper and the number on the building.

This is the right place; I'm here and I'm scared to death. What if they changed their minds? What if I have a terrible audition? My stomach is doing somersaults; it hurts like crazy.

Finally, I open the door and stride across the lobby to the receptionist's desk. My legs feel like jelly.

"Hello."

Suddenly, I can't swallow.

"I'm Paul."

"Can't you read? See the signs?"

"Excuse me?"

"End of the hallway, third door on the right! Just follow the arrows! Why is that so hard to understand?"

Then she goes back to talking, as if I'd already left.

"No way . . . I'll have to do that all day? I must be dreaming!"

". . . No, I'm here for the film . . ."

". . ."

"I'm an actor . . ."

". . ."

". . . Well, I'm an extra . . ."

"Oh? An actor? Great . . . In that case, end of the hallway, third door on the right!"

". . . Thank you . . ."

I leave the reception desk and head toward the hallway . . . then go back.

"Sorry, but where are the restrooms, please?"

"Same hallway, but at the very end, last door."

She looks me straight in the eyes.

"Leave it as clean as you found it, get it?"

"Umm . . ."

The pressure on my bladder is becoming unbearable. I start dancing in place.

"Go on!"

I walk a little faster to escape her view and especially to avoid hearing more of her comments. A few minutes later, after relieving myself, I'm ready to go again. Despite the risk of being late, I tell myself that I'll stay in the restroom just a bit longer to avoid running into that harpy. I immediately change my mind, though. The more time that passes, the more my presence in the stall becomes suspicious. Still not totally at ease, I force myself to smile and open the door with confidence. She's no longer at her desk. Phew. I'll bet she went to get a coffee. Probably her tenth cup this morning. That would explain why she is so on edge. Well, the path is clear; the dream-busters and killjoys are behind me now. I'm ready to become a part of the movie world. Totally pumped, I count the doors between myself and my dream that awaits.

What did she tell me? The first one? No, no . . . the third door. She said it's the third door. One . . . two . . . and three. I take a deep breath. I'm going to remember this moment for the rest of my life! I knock twice politely but nothing. I clear my throat, as if that will make my knock sound more confident. I look around me, but don't see anyone. I gather up my courage and knock loudly three times. Still no success. Well, that's disturbing. She told me it was the third door on the right, though. Don't panic; there must be a logical explanation. Take a deep breath, calm down, and think. She had no reason to lie to you . . .

I have absolutely no desire to go back and ask her again. I've already been humiliated enough for one day. I close my eyes. I focus and try to remember my every step since I arrived.

Hmm . . . Blah, blah, blah, OK, yes, then, blah, blah, blah . . . that's
it! It's that simple! I walked up from the end of the hallway; so,
it's not the door on the right where I should knock, but the one
on the left. Since I came from the opposite direction, I have to
switch sides! BINGO! I turn around to face the correct door. A
sheet of paper is lying on the ground with two strips of tape
at each end. It must not have been securely taped to the door.
I bend over and pick it up. It reads, "Enter without knocking."
I hear a sound in the entryway. The dragon lady must have
finished her coffee. Undeterred, I open the door and disappear
inside the room.

A young woman greets me.

"Hello, and welcome to There Can Be Only One Productions."

"Hello . . ."

I can't finish my sentence because she continues speaking.

"Please sit here and sign all the contracts we prepared for
you. Put your initials on each page and sign the last one. If you
have any questions, don't hesitate to ask!"

"Thank . . ."

"Have a seat. Here's a pen and some water. When you're
done, you'll continue on to the next rooms. Our medical staff will
be happy to verify that nothing will prevent you from taking this
adventure with us."

". . ."

"If you have any questions, don't hesitate to ask!"

I pick up a contract and act like I'm reading it, but just flip
through the pages.

"Put your initials on each page and sign the last one."

"Yes, yes . . ."

"Be sure that you have read everything, initialed, and signed, otherwise you would, unfortunately, not be able to join us on this incredible adventure that awaits you. That awaits us."

I nod my head in understanding. Twenty minutes later, I've finally finished my writing exercise. The pen is only on the table a second before the young woman waves me over.

"Great, now, don't forget to put your first and last name and address on these pre-stamped envelopes . . . Good . . . Now, please follow me. In the next room, over there, through that door, there is a stall. You can leave your things there. On the other side, a doctor will be waiting for you when you're ready."

She pauses and looks me up and down.

"To save time, remove your clothes down to your underwear."

I reach for the button on my jeans.

"Once you're inside, young man . . . inside. If you have any questions, don't hesitate to ask!"

I acknowledge her with a nervous nod.

"OK, I'll leave you to get ready. It won't be long."

I'm sitting in my underwear on three small boards meant to be a seat. My clothes hang on the hook behind me, taking up almost all the space. This situation is quite uncomfortable. I feel like I'm in line at the swimming pool, but there's no guarantee I'll be allowed to go play in it. A small bearded man, his face half-hidden behind huge glasses, finally opens the door and invites me into a large room. Inside, there are all kinds of machines with tubes and pumps, as well as a stationary bike and a treadmill . . . The only decoration consists of lots of cabinets, containing all

kinds of bottles and colorful substances. Without paying me any attention, he returns to the large, stuffed chair behind his desk. Once seated, he nods toward a chair across from him, signaling for me to sit down. He adjusts his glasses and starts reading a file. After a few minutes, he lifts his head just enough to gaze at me over his glasses. Then he breaks the silence.

"Any family history I should know about?"

"None. But I plan on changing that! That's why I'm here."

The doctor lets out a bored sigh while tapping his fingers on his desk. He appears to be gathering words in his head, but he doesn't know what order to put them in yet. He takes a deep breath and continues.

"Any allergies?"

I hesitate. I would say "to school," but now does not seem like the appropriate time for jokes.

"None."

"Any problem with needles or giving blood?"

"No . . ."

The doctor pushes a small tray over to me. It contains a tiny red pill and a miniature plastic cup filled with an unknown liquid.

"Perfect. Now, you'll start by taking this. It's a pill that will help you during your adventure. We will see how your body responds to our special medicine!"

After a one-hour physical, including stress tests, an electrocardiogram, and checking my blood pressure, vision, and hearing, the doctor tells me I can get dressed. He points to another room where one of his colleagues will be waiting for me for another interview. Before leaving the room, I turn around and ask him, "Is this a normal part of all film shoots?"

"Excuse me?"

"Do you do this every time with all the actors?"

"I don't know what you are talking about, young man. I do what they tell me to do, and that's it."

While I'm considering my response, the doctor opens the door to another stall to greet the next patient. I enter a different room, where a somewhat elderly woman is seated, also wearing gigantic glasses. By some kind of miracle, they seem to be balanced on the tip of her nose. I can't take my eyes off of them. Hanging from each side is a silver chain that appears to be keeping them reasonably secured. All the same, I have a deep desire to reach over and push them up on her nose so they don't fall. Then, she launches into a battery of questions:

Do you feel good about yourself?

Do you have any allergies, phobias, or family conditions?

Are you prone to negative thoughts?

Each time I respond, I see the tip of her pen scribble on the questionnaire. I also notice that, once she's reached the end, she continues with another question.

"Where's the beef?"

"Excuse me?"

Without blinking, she looks me in the eye, then breaks into a sinister laugh that sounds like it could have come from the Joker himself.

"Calm down, young man. It's a joke from a commercial that's almost as old as me! You and I are from different generations but that doesn't matter. We have finally finished! You may go home and rest. You'll need it! And don't worry, someone will contact you in a few days."

As I get up to leave and head toward the door, she shares one more thought with me.

"You know, it takes a lot of courage to do what you're doing; I've seen lots of people give up at the last minute."

She pauses and shoots me a warm smile.

"I doubt we will see each other again. So, good luck, young man!"

7

THE GREEN SCREEN OF HOPE

I slowly open my eyes. I can't believe it; I'm still on Small Island after that frightening storm! Maybe the pill I took during the test phase is the reason for this miracle. There are so many things here that don't make sense to me. Does that mean they all knew about this insane place where I was headed? What does this have to do with the movie? And with the extras? This makes no sense. It's all above my pay grade anyway; it's not like I had a choice. I'm a prisoner here, and I have to find a way to escape.

The crazy thing is that, despite everything that happened, the same flurry of dancing, shooting, and building is everywhere all around me on Small Island. I could almost get used to this constant frenzy. I'm starting to feel more at home here. That doesn't mean I'll forget my new goal: go back to the house where I found that huge camera. A film crew must have been working there at some point or another during the day. All I have to do is wait there and I'll run into someone eventually. As for the storm, I'll deal with that when I have to. I now know it exists, and my radio will alert me when it's coming. I won't be caught by surprise again! If I'm expecting it, I may have time to escape it by running in the right direction. I guess I'll find out soon enough.

Hunched down in my seat on the bus, I examine my map. According to my notes, we are not heading in the right direction to reach that house. It's going to take me a while to get back there. Nonetheless, I don't have a choice, really . . .

So, I have been soaring in the sky for several minutes. To pass the time, I look for shapes in Big Island's geography. I usually do this with the clouds. With a little focus, you can practically find a zoo in the sky. My sightings consist of elephants, triceratops, ants, and praying mantises. Before this adventure, I spent all of my time with both feet on the ground and not in the air, hanging from a handmade glider. I float over the big main lake. There is nothing exciting about it. In the dark and far away, it could be said that maybe it looks like a butterfly. A little to the north, an open pit forms the shape of an umbrella, more or less. I smile.

I'm flying over the biggest city on the island, where the impressive buildings are located and the incessant shootings take place, when my daydreams are interrupted. Explosions! Their intensity and proximity leaves little doubt where I am. I calculated my trajectory to keep a safe distance from this chaos. I'm not far from my destination. If everything goes as planned, I should land gracefully several yards from the fence around the house. Technically, I could just glide down right in front of the door, but even though manners seem to have deserted this part of the world, I follow a few of them anyway. Just in case . . .

My landing on the grass goes very smoothly. I hold my breath for several seconds to try to detect even the slightest sign of life. Apart from nature breathing, the area seems unoccupied. I empty my lungs and take a quick look through the windows.

Nothing and no one are around here. I jump over the fence and head toward the door. After two polite knocks and three hard ones on the wooden door, I decide to enter. Nothing has changed since the last time. I take my time to inspect the premises. They're dilapidated, poorly maintained . . . None of this bodes well for the next part. No need to spend more time on the ground floor, so I head for the basement. Here, too, there's no change; the green screen and equipment are just as I left them. Clearly, no one comes here anymore. It was just wishful thinking . . .

Disappointed, I fall heavily onto the couch. I hear a crack, causing me to freeze. If that was my spine, then I'm in trouble. I stare at my feet and try to move my toes. Phew . . . they work fine. I have an insanely difficult time extracting myself from this thing that now looks more like a futon than a sofa. It's as if invisible arms are holding me back. With a final bit of effort, I manage to get up. I turn around, ready to face this trap I just escaped. That's when I hear . . .

"CHHHHHH ••• THE STORM STARTS IN 59 SECONDS ••• CHHHHHH!"

Oops. Aha, one of the announcements that I missed last time! A weather alert. That is not what I would call good news, but that remains to be seen. I should leave as fast as possible and find a way to escape the storm again. I have no desire to repeat what happened yesterday.

There appears to be some kind of drawing sticking out where the couch is broken. I might have a chance to . . .

"CHHHHHH ... NARROWING IN 19 SECONDS ... CHHHHHH!"

I'm running out of time; I have to hurry. I pull apart the rest of the couch to dig out my treasure. Bingo! It's a drawing of a road, an enormous chair on one side, a tiny house on the other, and on the roof of the house there is a car. Completing the image is a giant tree perched on a hill. The artist did not sign it, but he did take the time to add a small compass in one corner. That symbol clearly indicates that this is a map, even though it may not appear to be one otherwise. Yes! The presence of an enormous red X, lightly sketched above the car-topped house, leaves no doubt. I didn't just find a regular map, but a treasure map!

"CHHHHHH ... THE EYE OF THE STORM IS SHRINKING ... CHHHHHH!"

These alerts are extremely unnerving. I have no idea what this mysterious X means, but I intend to find out! Did the film crew leave it there? Did someone like me leave a trail of clues behind pointing to an exit? Regardless, my intuition is correct. No matter how long it takes, I'll get out of here.

I just have to locate one of those three objects on the island and everything else will follow. The giant tree on a hill: skip it. There are too many of those around here. The chair: that depends on its size. It looks especially big in this drawing, but I have the feeling that the artist didn't pay much attention to proportions. On the other hand, a car on a roof! You cannot miss that!

"YOU'RE IN THE STORM: RUN!"

Noooo! I got caught again! I quickly run upstairs to leave the building. The rain drops sting my face, and I feel my energy being depleted. I dart like an arrow from one room to another, and finally reach the door. I find myself nose to nose with the two metal tubes of a shotgun. Everything stops inside me. My heart, my breathing, my hopes. A deafening explosion rings out. It's so powerful that I close my eyes.

When I decide to reopen them, the weapon, previously under my nostrils, is now lying at my feet. Its owner has disappeared and been replaced by a young girl who is looking straight into my eyes. Neither of us moves, despite the deluge. Under the intense flashes and lightning bolts, she pulls out a can of spray paint and sketches something on the ground. She leaps to turn away and starts running to escape the storm. Then, something utterly incredible happens. Under her feet, wooden boards appear. They form a ramp sloping up to the sky, pointing south. She must be a builder. While watching her get farther away in the purple light of the storm, she suddenly disappears with a very strange sound. The explosion hits me like an electric shock and I finally regain contact with reality. I have to get moving. Maybe I have enough time to escape, too. I hurry after her. However, I stop immediately and examine the mark she made before leaving. It's a cluster of small red hearts.

Wow! What does it mean? First, she saves my life, then she leaves me a message? It could just be her signature. After all, tags are only names, or drawings to mark one's territory, not personal messages. I'm suffocating in this violent storm. I won't survive long if I keep standing here. I follow her path. I'm a little bit scared of climbing the ramp, but do I really have any other choice? Despite the worrisome cracking sounds of the wood under my feet, the planks seem to hold my weight. I'm getting higher and higher.

The ramp finally ends at a small platform containing a strange device. It looks like a solid disc, fairly thick and embedded in the planks with four feet. Its edges, with cables hanging from them, are dotted in small lights. The entire thing looks like a teleportation device. My legs start to wobble . . . Could this be an exit to the real world? Will I finally be free? Despite the rain and storm, it's hard to say, but I think tears are forming in my eyes.

On one, two . . . I jump in a way that lands me as close as possible to the device's center.

Uh oh, the thing reacts like an Olympic springboard. With the sound of pressure being released and springs expanding, it shoots me into the air at a mind-blowing speed. In a moment of panic I accidentally open my glider. The speed, combined with the direction of my jump, shoots me upward, and in just a few seconds, away from the chaos of the bad weather. I'm now flying in open space, leaving the storm behind me. I glide around to observe it. My perspective offers me an unobstructed view and helps me understand three things about how it operates. First, it acts a bit like a cyclone. The center is a safe zone, where you can breathe normally. Second, it changes place around the island. Finally, and most discouragingly, the center shrinks as time passes.

The storm's center provides the most security. Is the toxic cloud cleared out by a fan or something like that? Or maybe there's a vacuum involved? If the big red X on the drawing does not indicate a treasure, could it have been the location of one of these vent systems? I absolutely must solve this riddle; this could be my passport to freedom!

While considering all of this, I inspect the area. I need a quiet place to land. To my right, a majestic tree looms on top of a hill. Lower down, an imposing iron bridge crosses one of the rivers cutting the island in two. Small cabins are located at each end of this structure. To the south, I can make out a factory, and in front of me, I spot an isolated residence on a cliff. That is where I decide to land.

I wonder who that girl was who saved me earlier. She was the spitting image of the girl who usually stands on the H at the helicopter pad on Small Island. If that's the same girl, then something strange is going on. Which group does she belong to? I was sure she was a standstill . . . but to build that ramp, so fast and effectively . . . that's the work of a builder. It would be impossible for that to be the same person.

While still floating in the air, I see a new building suddenly appear. And there's the girl again! With impressive speed and agility, she heads toward the house on the rocky clifftop. There is no doubt that she will get there before I do. All of a sudden, I hear the sound of a rocket launcher behind me. As I turn around to try to see exactly what's happening, a rocket shoots by just below my feet! Someone inside the cabins next to the bridge just fired it. How awful! I see what he is trying to do. If the projectile reaches the house before she's inside, she'll never survive the fall . . . Fortunately, like me, she heard the explosion and already built an exit ramp, separate from the first one. At its highest point, she continues by quickly creating a shelter, and then she immediately retaliates. One blast later, the threat has been eliminated, and now she heads toward the house again.

Because of my stupid attempt to turn around, I lost track of time and altitude. I'll never make it to her and the clifftop in time. No, no, no, no . . . I crash into the rock wall and slide pathetically down to the bottom. I feel weaker, but still able to go on.

"CHHHHHH ... THE EYE OF THE STORM IS SHRINKING ... CHHHHHH!"

Oh no! The storm is moving again and is approaching fast! Unfortunately, the ramp is not usable since the rocket destroyed it. I don't have a choice; I have to bypass the clifftop. I hope I can find her on the other side. All right, here we go!

8

BUILDING A BETTER WORLD

I run like a madman with the storm at my heels. The perimeter of the rocky mountain that I'm trying to bypass is irregular, like ice cream when a spoon has been dipped in several places. Inside one of the recesses, I discover another ramp. Someone approaching from the south clearly climbed to the summit from this side. If I use it, I might be in danger of running into trouble. Still, this structure provides a shortcut to escape the storm and it just might help me see the young girl again. I shoot up the steps two at a time. These are made of stone, and are more solid and well crafted than those I'd used before now. I look behind me to judge how far I am from the storm. Then I stop ascending because it's stopped moving along its destructive path. Perfect. But for how long, I have no idea. I have to depend on the alerts to tell me when I'll be moving again. I start ascending again but slower this time. Something tells me I'm not climbing a stairway to heaven.

I miss a lot of things, including music. This entire episode has been stressful. A few songs—or just the chorus of some of my favorites—would really help me relax . . .

Finally, I reach the summit, but it seems a little too calm. In front of me proudly stands a little hut next to a single-story house with an enormous chimney. To my right lies a container in the grass, in the middle of nowhere. How did that get here? A very simple question, but it's extremely unsettling. It casts doubt on my theory of where the supplies are stored. If this box fell from a shipment during a delivery, that would mean the supplies arrive by air, not from underground. Grrr! This is all starting to get on my nerves. The moment I develop a theory, I get new information that shatters it into a thousand pieces.

Farther away, on the left at the cliff's edge, someone created half of a basketball court. That's cool! I would have loved to have that back home. Even though, personally, I would not have chosen that location. Apart from two wooden fences, nothing was installed to prevent the ball from going over the edge. If you miss a pass or a shot, say goodbye to your ball. What a nightmare it would be to get it back! I ignore the cabin for now and go visit the house. Several partial structures, spread all over the place, have been built in a disorderly fashion. One of the house's walls, like the roof, has been gutted, suggesting a wild battle took place here.

I stop for several seconds to listen. The longer I'm here, the more I realize that a sound can tell you a lot about a situation. Apart from the wind, nothing disturbs the peace and quiet of this location. I continue my reconnaissance mission and end up finding . . . an ice cream truck!

"CHHHHHH ... THE EYE OF THE STORM
IS SHRINKING ... CHHHHHH!"

Yikes, the storm is on the move! I get that someone wanted to live like a hermit on a mountaintop, but why—and how in the world—did they have an ice cream truck delivered here? I feel like more surprises are just waiting around the corner . . .

I have to move and I don't have any other choice but to go south. I leave the house behind me. I pass by the container; its doors are wide open. It's empty. A little farther along, at the edge of the cliff, someone built a wooden platform resembling a dock. I can easily see planes landing here to deliver merchandise or offload passengers . . . but that doesn't help much. Either the deliveries are made by air, which casts doubt on my theory about the underground tunnels, or they're made using ramps that disappear afterward. Though the wood is too flimsy to hold a truck, the stone seems much sturdier. There is a good chance that the structures I have seen built are the missing link. That would help explain, a little more rationally, some of the strange events that take place on both islands.

"YOU'RE IN THE STORM: RUN!"

I'm standing at the edge with the wind and rain already knocking me around. How will I get down from here? I lean forward to take a look at the rock wall. I think I see a ledge farther down. If I can slide to it, I may be able to descend, little by little, without getting hurt too much. I just have to . . . Aahhhhh! My foot slips on the dock's wet boards. I go tumbling all the way down the steep slope. My movements are totally uncontrolled. I just do what I can to grab anything that comes within reach. I don't know whether I bumped into something or pressed something in my backpack accidentally, but I see partial structures appear above me, then alongside me. Nothing helps; I can't slow my descent. I'm not even sure if I caused those boards to appear . . . I end up smashing into the ground and passing out after a frightening, loud thud.

. . .

I slowly open my eyes and realize I'm back on Small Island. I'm almost positive I built those partial ramps. There was no one around, and those planks appeared during my fall. There can't be any other explanation. So I was mistaken about the people here. Some people are experts in dancing, others shooting or building, but that doesn't mean that others can't learn to do it all. I have to find out how to build.

I sneak up behind some builders to observe them. I have to admit that it doesn't help much. Apparently, there is no single, specific gesture; the shapes appear on their own around the builders. I fiddle with my bag, trying to pretend to build a staircase, hoping to set off its creation, but nothing happens. What's their secret? The only thing I haven't used yet is a small pickaxe that they handed us all when we arrived. But the people building structures don't use it! The ones who use that tool are attacking a tree, building, or some other object with it for about ten seconds, then moving on to something else.

"THE COMBAT BUS LEAVES IN TEN SECONDS!"

During the trip, I decide that the best thing I can do is to isolate myself somewhere on Big Island and try to do something with my hands. I'm not giving up on my treasure map, but for now, I have to recognize that being able to build bridges, or even basic ramps, would make my exploration of the area much more effective.

Several minutes later, I land about ten yards from the house opposite Small Island. The one with the balcony facing inland instead of toward the sea. That's pretty funny when I think about it. I take the time to look around me to see whether any "residents" decided to land in the area. Evidently, there's no one. So I go back to the building and down to the basement, away from any lurking eyes. I take out my pickaxe and attack a wooden drum lying in the corner. One hit and it explodes into pieces. Strangely, there's nothing left. Even though that was a bit noisy, I think I'm far enough underground to not attract attention. I'll be able to continue. I attack several boards that cover the staircase.

I'm too far from my target, and end up just slicing through the air, like a fan blade. Once I'm in a better spot, the wood disappears with hardly any effort. All at once, I demolish everything around me. It's a great feeling.

Wow! I scared myself. I just destroyed an old electric meter that shot out sparks as it died. I have a tendency to get carried away without considering the consequences. You've gotta learn from your mistakes, I guess. The only thing still standing in the basement is an old water heater. So I'll leave it alone.

I attack the stairway. It's one hundred percent wood, no danger there. My movements become more fluid, I even let myself move around on a path of destruction. Oh my god, it works! Everything has disappeared, except the water heater, of course. Quite proud of myself, I look around the room. Now that it's the only thing left, I feel like it's taunting me. Not for long! I leap into the air with my pickaxe and WHACK! I attack the object with my eyes closed. My bravery has limits though, so I open one eye, then the other. This time, the room is truly empty. I take a deep breath, happy with my work. Then, suddenly, concern washes over me . . . How will I get back upstairs since I destroyed the staircase? Gulp. I now have proof that I'm better with my hands than my brain, as if I needed it.

Jumping frantically, I try my best to grab hold of the flooring above me to pull myself up. No luck. I had broken it all. Now I have no way out of here. How could I have been so stupid? Stuck again; the best I can do is stand back. So I take a few steps back to assess the situation. As I clutch the two straps on my backpack, like a student would on his way to school, it appears. My first ramp. At first, it's a hologram. Surprised, I squeeze my hands tighter. Accompanied by a construction-type sound, it materializes in a few seconds. Incredible. I was right! I can create things. A sense of satisfaction and power overcomes me. I turn around and make another item appear on the ceiling, then another behind it, then nothing. I yank the straps with the same conviction I would use to milk a cow, but the system no longer responds. Without panicking, I decide to get myself out of this rat hole before things get worse. You can never be too careful.

Once I'm out in the open, I make sure there's no one around. Then I hide behind the house to find some quiet. Two grand trees stand proudly over me, while in the distance, I can spot Small Island. I try to reproduce the construction miracle. Still no reaction. I start to get mad. Why doesn't anything work the way I want it to!? Full of rage, I attack the two trees with the pickaxe. I manage to make them disappear without feeling the least bit fatigued. The view is now entirely unobstructed. I wonder how much distance there is between the two islands. Would it be possible to construct a ramp large enough to connect them? People are always on one island or the other . . . but what would happen if I managed to enter that zone where no one lives? I would surely see the delivery routes for supplies. Without a doubt, that would be the perfect time to . . . Well, before that, I have to figure out how to build these stupid structures! Then, something incredible happens, overriding my thoughts: when I mechanically squeeze the straps of my backpack, the ramp hologram reappears!

How could I have been so stupid? The difference between now and awhile ago is my fit of anger I took out on the environment! The pickaxe allows me to collect raw materials, which my equipment then uses. So, when I run out of materials, it's adios structures . . .

I circle the house. There are stones just begging to be used. Is my tool sturdy enough for this type of work? In just seconds, I've become a criminal. The stone disappears almost as fast as the wood. As soon as I'm done, I squeeze the straps. It doesn't work. I yank them in various directions. Without really understanding how, I manage to change the shapes, angles, and, suddenly BINGO! I went from one material to the other! Aha! Freedom is close!

If I want to make bigger structures, I'll need to collect lots of material. To avoid strangers, I'll follow the coast, clearing out everything I see. Before long, they'll be calling me the Attila the Hun of the environment. My collecting journey takes me south, into a very hilly area. I decide to climb to a small ridge with a gorgeous view, as well as plenty of resources. I arrive in no time, gather a large amount of wood, then stand still for a moment, admiring the view.

A bit to the east, a majestic tree looms on the very top of a mountain. Below to the south, I see a dilapidated house, and a bit farther along, between these two, a few evergreens barely conceal a group of buildings.

"YOU'RE IN THE STORM: RUN!"

Oh no! I wasn't paying attention. I must have been so busy using the pickaxe, I didn't hear the previous messages. Now, it's a race. The summit I saw seems to be my best option. Once I'm there, I should be safe for a few minutes. During my descent, I notice immense scaffolding in front of the entrance to the inhabited area. It has a platform on top, but I can't figure out what its purpose might be. I have to move fast if I'm going to

avoid fainting. I pass a tiny cabin containing a television that was left on, with static filling the screen.

Questions run through my head, while my reasoning and instincts tell me to run. At the foot of the mountain, I yank on my backpack. The hologram of the upward slope appears and I quickly construct a wonderful ramp. I start climbing, but then I realize I've made a terrible mistake. My ramp ends halfway up the hill. I should have started it farther up with less of an incline. To escape the storm, I have to reach the summit, no matter what! I don't feel well. I have to change the direction of my boards and create connecting pieces to reach the other side. Then I'll be able to climb up again.

Suddenly, I hear a sound that I don't like. Below me, my first structure is crumbling. Someone is riddling my creation with bullets. Quick, to the top . . . QUICK! Before everything disappears! The bullets splinter the wood, which falls apart quickly. While I run at full speed toward the summit, the last planks give way under my assailant's gunshots. My fall is inevitable.

9

GUT FEELING

Thwack . . .

While bullets continue whizzing past me, I fall in the most humiliating way possible. Now at the end of my connecting ramp, I realize that I was just above the mountaintop when I started to fall. I must have fallen from just within a foot of the top!

Now crouched down, I scurry to hide behind an immense tree. Its unusual shape reminds me of a mushroom. I hesitate to destroy it, because it does offer protection after all. The attack finally ends. I have to decide fast. The storm will start moving again soon, and it could be hard to escape from everyone all at once.

I make a fence hologram appear. The shots seem to have come from the houses. I get close to the edge to check. If they start again, I'll build a makeshift shelter in the blink of an eye. That will leave me enough time to reach my real shelter, safe and sound. I slowly continue forward. Everything is calm. My speaker starts shouting:

"CHHHHHH ... NARROWING IN 3 MINUTES AND 19 SECONDS ... CHHHHHH!"

Pressed for time, I have to plan how to get down from my perch. I see no suspicious movements. On the other hand, I now see the large structure at the entrance to the inhabited area from a different angle. From here, I notice that it's absolutely not scaffolding! It's a chair! A giant chair. If that's the one I think it is, then . . .

My gaze settles directly on the houses and a car balances on the roof of one of them. Stuck with the front end among the shingles, the vehicle is indeed there. Excellent! I finally located some of the items on the treasure map! Oh jeez, I should have noted the exact location of that big red X . . . If my memory is correct, it's got to be around there, down below, under an evergreen. I'll have to search through the entire area using my pickaxe, but the attacker nearby will make that difficult. One thing at a time. First, I have to leave my perch. I'm going to try to find a route on the back side so that I attract as little attention as possible. To the east, the peak's slope is less steep than everywhere else. Plus, a rocky outgrowth could serve as a refuge if a problem arises. I should be able to slide down without hurting myself. I'll save my ability to build structures as a tool in my tool belt in case the situation gets worse. I approach the edge. Then, taking a deep breath, I lean as far back as possible and let gravity carry me away. At first, with my hands, then my entire body, I slow my fall the best I can. I finally reach the natural platform in a poof of dust. I crouch down again and lean forward to review the situation around the houses.

"CHHHHHH ... THE EYE OF THE STORM IS SHRINKING ... CHHHHHH!"

Already?! The moment the alert goes out, I see the shooter emerge from behind the fence surrounding the car-topped house. He quickly leaps out of my field of vision like a goat. He received the same alerts I did. But rather than lying in ambush, he decided it was better to run. The path is clear. Not much time remains, just enough to find the evergreen marked with a red X on the treasure map. To reach the ground, I have to slide down on my back again. The slope doesn't seem any steeper, just a little longer. I can do this! I wouldn't do it any differently than if I were sledding down. I let myself drop. My body gets hotter and hotter as I take on speed. The friction intensifies and the dust forms a real cloud around me. I can't tell if it's the adrenaline from my descent, or the fear of the storm coming toward me, but I still feel no pain. I make it down without a problem, landing on the path around the foot of the mountain. Across from me, on a small hill, a majestic evergreen stands tall. A few strides farther and I arrive quickly under its branches. I instantly pull out my pickaxe because, in less than ten seconds, I'll be overcome by the blue gas. I don't need much time to destroy the tree and find out what it's hiding. One strike. Two strikes. With the third, it disappears in a large halo of light that completely blinds me. I hear thunderous shouts and applause, followed by a sharp whistle. As fast as they occurred, the sounds end all at once. In a few seconds, I come to my senses. I have a hard time breathing. I'm in the storm. I look at my feet. I look around me. Nothing changed. Nothing moved. Just a flash and a sensation like I was in a stadium. No way, that's not possible. There must be something else. I did not do all of that just to be struck by lightning! I want to give up, even though I know it will not change a thing. I have to get myself out.

After several seconds, despite the disappointment, I'm back at it. I'm in the storm and I can't stay there. So I start running toward the river. The whole time, I don't feel well. It's not the gas, but something else . . . It feels like I'm gradually losing control of my head. I swallow as much as I can, rub my eyes . . . Nothing helps. I cross the water's slow-moving current and then realize that I'm finally outside of the poisonous cloud. A strange sense of fear overcomes me. I feel like someone—or something—is watching me. More toward the south and behind a tree, I spot a small wooden cabin. It would make the perfect plank. I have to stop and review my situation.

A few miles from there . . .

This cramped room doesn't allow in any natural light. The only lighting comes from about ten control screens, showing men and women moving around Big Island. Some are in the storm, others are not.

Here, in this television control room, everyone is busy, but behind one large console, an operator is panicking. He presses a series of buttons. His eyes are riveted on the indicator lights.

"What's going on? This is impossible! The live camera went out in the recording system . . ."

One of his colleagues stands up and looks over his shoulder.

"What are you talking about?"

"I don't know why, but there was a problem with the player's sound. Something strange happened with the console when he found the secret. There was loud feedback. The contestant may have even heard the audience in the stadium on his radio."

"No!"

"I swear to you . . ."

While no other technicians are paying attention to this conversation, a man storms into the room. He's wearing a black jacket and a T-shirt with the slogan "No Future" scribbled across it.

"What was that howling sound, guys?! We look like a bunch of amateurs!"

"It was just feedback. I'm on it . . . but I don't understand how it happened . . ."

"Whether you're on it, under it, or next to it, I really don't care! I want this to work! Period! There are fifteen guys like you behind this door who want to be in your seat, OK? This can't happen again!"

As fast as he entered, he left again. Only a few seconds later, the door reopens. The same man, still annoyed, sticks his head in to add:

"This is the most demanding, craziest, biggest reality television program ever created! You are the best. That's why you're here! Now prove it! The whole country is watching us, the world is watching us, and I'm watching YOU!"

Speech finished, he slams the door shut.

One hour later, in a meeting room . . .

His head in his hands, the man in the black jacket sits in the middle of a spacious room. A handful of co-workers surround him, all very absorbed in their tablets and smartphones. In front of him, a giant screen displays graphs, percentages, and all sorts of numbers related to the different residents on the two islands. The mass of data includes a photo of Paul. A young intern with glasses presents a report about the audiences, votes, and revenue generated by the various events on Big Island. The man in the black jacket finally sits up and stares at Paul's face on the giant screen. He interrupts the report.

"Who is that guy?"

A young woman instantly stands up, swipes her tablet with a finger twice in one direction, once in another, and then responds, "A wimp."

"Excuse me?"

"A wimp, a newbie, a nobody. But not a small one . . . A big wimp. Since the beginning, he hasn't shot at anyone . . ."

"What's he doing there?"

The young woman taps on her screen faster.

"He went through the normal selection process. No sponsor, no specific recommendations, nothing."

"And this nobody found the bonus on the treasure map before everyone else?"

"Technically, he's the third to find it . . ."

The man in the black jacket inhales deeply and drops his head back into his hands. Everyone around the table turns serious. The casualness that initially filled the room has completely disappeared. He speaks again.

"This guy has not shot even one other person since the beginning? Nothing?"

"The stats show that he hasn't even shot one bullet."

There is a long, awkward silence. The tension goes up a notch in the meeting room. Everyone waits to hear the decision.

"I bet you one hundred dollars that he's a journalist, or something like that. This guy thinks he's a big reporter and wants to ruin our show from the inside! I want a complete report on him right away. I want to know everything! He wants to play? We're going to play, he can count on that."

He stands and, before disappearing, adds, "And no focus on him during prime time, OK? He collected the bonus points from the map. Great, we can mention that, but I don't want to see his winning face on the episodes, is that clear? Well, as little as possible . . ."

One hour later . . .

Relieved of his jacket, the man lounges in a chair behind a desk. He's on the phone, eyes closed, files, brochures, and magazines spread out before him.

"Yeah . . . yeah. I don't understand. You're sure that he didn't touch a single weapon? You reviewed all the videos? All of them?"

Then, after a long minute without a word, he sits up to search through an open file in front of him.

"Before he found the bonus, no one mentioned him, right? Good. The networks are a little worked up; that's to be expected. That always happens with the player who finds the next little prize or wins best shooter."

He pauses again, then adds, "OK . . . you know what, I don't care about that. Don't let him out of your sight. I want you to watch his every move. When even the smallest thing happens I want to know. For the next prime time episode, put the spotlight on the Angel of Death. Get me something on him, anything. Invent a sentence he would have said or doctor up a photo if you have to. I want him to be the center of the world. We'll start a counterattack for sure."

He hangs up the phone and, one last time, skims over the file in front of him before closing it. Alone in his office, he speaks to the photo of Paul on the front page.

"I don't know who you are, but I'm going to find out. You think you can blow up our system from the inside? Well, I'm going to turn you into nothing but a water balloon that makes a measly splat when it bursts."

10

THE BIG GAME

All the lights are out in the stadium. It's decorated like a fighting arena. A timer counts down on the giant screen. In the audience, thousands of people, going wild, count out loud as the numbers scroll by. At zero, as rock music blares and a blinding light show covers the stadium, a man appears in the sky. He holds a revolver-shaped microphone in his right hand, pointing it at the camera filming him. With his left hand, he pretends to be hanging from an enormous umbrella and delicately steps onto the enormous stage. Once both feet touch the ground, he makes his way to the edge of the platform to address the crowd.

He shouts, "*Battle for!*"

The crowd responds, "*Domination!*"

"I can't hear you! *Battle for!*"

"*Domination!*"

"*BATTLE FOR!*"

"*DOMINATION!*"

"Good evening! Good evening to you all, our growing audience who, each week, joins us in the battle dome . . ."

He turns toward one of the many cameras on the stage.

"And good evening to those of you in the even bigger audience watching on your screens!"

Suddenly, he disappears from the stage, vanishing into a trapdoor. The stage plunges into darkness again while a trailer for the game plays. A voice with so much bass that it vibrates the entire stadium introduces the context and rules, one by one. Each of his sentences is written on the gigantic screen. The audience sees images of the faces of several participants, the bus, some gliders, and landmarks from the two islands.

"There are one hundred. They agreed to face the craziest challenge ever imagined in the most extreme conditions a person has ever experienced. They don't know each other, they cannot talk to each other, but they all have the same goal: win the jackpot that will change their life forever! Forget manners, forget morals, forget all the rules. Only one thing counts: there can be only one. When they started the adventure, we filled the players' jackpot with a good amount to start. With each game, the top ten are paid. The closer they are to number one, the more they get."

"Woooow!"

"But be careful, the last fifty will be penalized. The more they lose, the more they have to shell out . . ."

"Ohhhh . . ."

"As for the winner, we are doubling the prize!"

After that announcement, the crowd goes wild. The lights come back up on the host. Now standing behind an impressive control panel that looks like a spaceship, with the ease of an orchestra conductor, he pretends to operate the lights and sounds for the show.

"Something amazing awaits us tonight on the new episode of *Battle for Domination*. This show is mine, theirs, and yours! All night long, you'll vote for your favorite contestant, the one you want to see win. Vote for the best action, the best shot, the wildest costume, the most crushing humiliation. VOTE! We are counting on you, and they're counting on you! Tons of prizes to win and the possibility of getting a percentage of your champion's jackpot, if he or she wins and decides to leave! To help you make the right choice, here is a recap of the most incredible action scenes from this week."

The lights go down again on the stage. For several minutes, the giant screen displays a montage of shooting, building, and dancing sequences. The audience erupts in wild laughter as the video plays.

"Are you ready?"

The crowd roars.

"I can't hear you . . . Are you ready? Are you ready to experience a new level of savage competition? Tonight, let's watch the freedom level!"

A round of applause overtakes the crowd.

"The winner of this unique episode can decide to stay in the game to increase his jackpot, or leave this incredible adventure for good with all of his winnings!"

The host pauses. Looking into the camera, a broad grin fills his face. Then he turns to the audience and, with a serious, almost solemn air, declares, "Dressed in black from head to toe. Everywhere he goes, he spreads chaos and destruction. Since our last show, everyone has called him the Angel of Death. Here is last week's winner!"

On the screen, a silhouette appears. His head, hidden by a black hood, is ringed by a crown of crow's feathers. It's impossible to distinguish any of his facial features. His eyes alone are visible and glow an eerie violet color. An electric current suddenly shoots through the atmosphere, while the crowd experiences mixed reactions of fear, admiration, and excitement.

"Without a second thought, he decided to stay. Let's see if our hero will once again successfully decimate the other players and have a chance to decide his own fate! Something tells me he will not be leaving any time soon. We recovered a tweet that he thought he'd deleted . . . I'll let you enjoy it!"

A message unfurls across the giant screen. Any information that could identify the author is illegible, but the rest reads, "I'm not doing this for the money; I'm already a millionaire. I enjoy humiliating the weaklings and the wimps. No one will leave until I say so. I'm a living god!"

The audience goes wild. However, the host quickly gets them under control using sound and light effects.

"My friends, my friends! Our champion is self-assured; that's not a bad thing! Reward yourself, reward US: VOTE! Vote for his competitors if you find him intolerable. Vote for him if you think he's amazing! Now, it's time to fly to the island of danger, the island of sacrifices. It's time for a new round of *BATTLE FOR!*"

"*DOMINATION!*"

Filmed by several cameras, the flying bus suddenly appears on the screen. The crowd shouts even louder when the first players leap out into the sky. Then, the contestants who made it to the top ten last week are presented in a special montage: some simultaneously in a large grid, some individually by going from one player to the next. The host pointedly analyzes every scene, predicting the players' actions. Whether it's a manhunt in an urban environment or gathering provisions in an isolated house, he always creates an event, building expectations.

"That's genius! Watch this hunting technique. He baits his prey to take refuge in the basement of the building. The very same basement that he filled with traps when he arrived!"

With loud mechanical sounds, the counter for the winning player increases as his jackpot increases, and the crowd cheers.

Throughout the first five minutes, the counters are constantly shifting. More than half of the participants have disappeared by this time.

"That's it! They were bad, they have to . . ."

"Pay!"

"They do indeed have to pay. The game is cruel, but that's life. Here is the list of payers."

Now, the screen displays the list of the last fifty participants. Next to each name appears the sum they will have to pay out, as well as the amount left in their jackpot. A siren sounds.

"What's going on?"

The audience starts chanting,

"The storm! The storm! The storm!"

"Yes, my friends! It's time for the storm! Who will be smart enough to avoid being taken by surprise? Who will be able to beat its destructive power and grab a few weapons, some ammunition, or building materials? Now is the time you'll get the answer to all of those questions!"

A drone films the toxic cloud's formation and shows the direction it's headed. The show now focuses on the cloud taking the players by surprise. The raucous crowd releases a wave of taunts and insults at the participants.

"Look at that wimp run . . . Oh! Too late . . . And watch that one! He may still set up a springboard. That would certainly let him escape. Oh! Uh oh, another player is shooting at the ramp he just built. It's crashing to the ground. It's over!"

For several minutes, the ambiance is electric. Another alert goes out.

"Do you know what that means, my friends? There are only ten people left in the running. No matter what happens from now on, they're already winners! Their jackpot, like the itsy bitsy spider, keeps climbing higher and higher . . ."

In the middle of the safe zone, the Angel of Death builds a colossal metal tower. He stacks up floors with disturbing speed and builds a gigantic platform on the very top. Various observation posts protect it from potential shooters. The height gives him an advantage over the other competitors. None of them dares intervene while he develops what now looks like a fort. Once his structure is complete, the crowd's favorite grabs a sniper rifle quickly. The audience now sees on the screen exactly the same thing as the contestant. Instead of shooting them down one by one, he takes his time and locates each of his adversaries. Without a word, just the movements of the sight and the zoom on his rifle, he clearly indicates their position, then takes it one step further. He seems to be predicting their strategies and future movements.

Suddenly, everything comes together. After locating all the other players, he leaves his observation post and sneaks up on his prey, defeating them one by one. Some are trickier than others, but the result is always the same: he gets them in the end, every time. The host, the audience, everyone explodes after each of his victories. Once he defeats the last player, fireworks light up the sky above the stadium. The final duel replays over and over on the giant screen.

"He did it! My friends, I don't know if I can still call him a man! He is a war machine, a god! The Angel of Death, for the second time in a row, has won the special level! Come back after the commercial break to find out what he decides to do. Will he leave? Will he stay? You still have a few minutes to vote and you might be the next one to participate in the *Battle for Domination!*"

During the break, thanks to a subtle play of light, the dashboard disappears from the stage, without anyone noticing. Again, using a trap door, the host explodes back onto the stage.

"He entertained us all night, but will he still be there next week to try again? The decision is up to him alone. Let's head over to the participants' room to talk to him!"

A gigantic door with a huge lock on it appears on the big screen. As the door opens, there is a sound of air decompressing. A camera moves inside to reveal an immense hangar. It looks like a science fiction set: everything is white except on the sides, which contain extensive control panels covered in buttons, indicator lights, and small flat screens. Men in protective suits are sitting behind desks working without noticing the camera that continues up the middle aisle. The aisle is lined with dozens of boxes, one after another, all linked together by sophisticated devices.

On the stage, the host speaks with an almost religious tone.

"Ladies and gentlemen, allow me to remind you of the rule: if our winner wants to leave, the green light will go on. Our medical teams will take over and bring him back to join us. But if the winner wants to continue increasing his jackpot, the red light will come on. Then he will be sent back to join the others and continue playing the game!"

Both lights start blinking. One time. Two times. Three times. Only the red light remains lit.

"He's staying! That's incredible; he's still in the game! Who will possibly dethrone him? Who will be good enough to be number one next week? How many more times will the Angel of Death humiliate his adversaries? Join us next week to find out. Until then, don't forget to watch our daily episodes and follow each player's ranking and changing jackpot. They play twenty-four hours a day, seven days a week for your enjoyment. We'll see you soon for another episode of *Battle for . . .*"

"Domination!"

"BATTLE FOR!"

"DOMINATION!"

11

GROCERY CART ICARUS

Far away in the southwest area of Big Island, I continue gathering lots of wood, stone, and anything I can find. While my pickaxe destroys everything it touches, I realize that I have no idea how much time has passed since the treasure map fiasco. I was so convinced that would be a valuable discovery. I didn't expect it to point me to the exit, but I did expect it to at least give me a big head start on my quest. Also, since that flash, I feel like I'm constantly being watched. I look over my shoulder when I'm running. I inspect the walls and ceilings as soon as I enter a house. I keep my ears open for the slightest sound. I don't know if I'm becoming paranoid or if I acquired certain survival skills. Probably some of both. For example, an open door is no longer an invitation to enter. It's quite the opposite. It means someone went through there. He or she could be inside still. So the best plan is to cross that person's path as discreetly as possible.

Not everything is negative. I ended up finding intact boxes in certain houses and outdoors. Easy to break open, they don't require a lock-pick. However, when they open, a small explosion is triggered that could attract the attention of any bystanders. This requires a certain level of caution. That risk is worth it, though, even if the box usually only contains weapons.

Those don't interest me. I would even go so far as to say I hate them. However, they also contain construction materials and survival kits. Those are very important, especially in case I fall or get caught in the storm. Besides, during my trips between the two islands, I noticed something interesting about these boxes: they always appear in the same places. They're a little bit like watering holes in the desert: everyone goes there to benefit from them and seek comfort, but they run the risk of encountering a battle there, too.

So, with time, I cultivate my understanding of this strange place. While I catch my breath in a small cabin near the river, and control my initial disappointment about the treasure map, I realize that my knowledge is reaching its limits when it comes to the storm. It must be hiding a lot more than I think. What kind of system runs it? Fuels it? Guides its movements? How does it change over time? I have so many questions and now I need to find the answers.

Excited by this new task ahead of me, I set out again to look for an observation post. I quickly set my sights on a beautiful, somewhat isolated, elevated area in the southern part of Big Island. The location is bursting with resources, all available for me to use. Arriving there, I look for the ideal spot to build a tower, and I discover something quite unexpected: a shopping cart. Exactly the same kind they have in stores. The frame is steel, easy to push, and light and sturdy at the same time. After standing there surprised a few seconds, I feel a twinge of sadness. I see myself with my father in a department store parking lot, playing pirates with my ghost ship on wheels.

Everything comes back to me: the sound of the wheels on the asphalt, the vibrations of the metal reverberating through my body, the sense of speed and power . . . Drowning in this wave of nostalgia, I feel the need to sit under a tree for a few minutes. Opposite me, a good distance away, I can distinctly see the cliffs of Small Island. That's when a wild idea hits me. What if I built a ski jump? One to rival those used in the Olympics for the skiing competitions. Would I be able to go from one island to another without fainting? By using the system against itself, I could surely find a way to get out of here! I know this plan may sound completely stupid, but it can't hurt to try. Aren't the craziest ideas the ones that produce the most incredible technological breakthroughs? The first plane, the first submarine, electricity . . . I'll become the first man to fly in a shopping cart! One small step for mankind, but a giant leap for me!

That's how I end up searching for all the necessary resources to build an enormous ski jump to send us, my shopping cart and me, to Small Island. What goes on over there, while everyone is on Big Island? I have to verify all the activities over there: deliveries, refueling, and anything that might provide an exit out of this awful place. Two key limitations face me: I cannot be taken by surprise while I'm building, because that will make me easy prey, and I have to keep myself far from the storm. I've got to be fast.

That's it. I destroy everything around me. Unless I continue farther inland, I won't be able to gather more resources. That would not be worthwhile . . . and way too risky. I only need a few seconds to build a first ramp starting in the elevated area and pointing toward my target. Once that's done, I add a stone platform to the end. I need it to be as sturdy as possible, since it will be my starting point. Once again, I build quickly. It doesn't need to be very wide. By reflex, I glance around me. Nothing moves; everything is calm. Perfect. I descend again to get my cart. I arrive back at my starting point with it and jam it in a corner to make sure it doesn't fall before everything is built. Next, I tackle the first part of my runway. Once the sections are lined up end to end, they form a long descent toward the ocean. Having jumped from the flying bus many times, vertigo has less of an effect on me now. I have to admit that I'm very pleased with myself, perched there out in the open, building my ramp. As I repeat the same movement, my work speeds up. In a few seconds, I'll be able to move on to the second part of my ski jump. Uh oh! I don't have enough rocks. So I make the rest out of wood. I cross my fingers, hoping that this will not affect my rolling descent in the cart at full speed. Next, I tackle the horizontal section. I realize, to my dismay, that I have no way to create a smooth transition between the different parts of my structure. Oh well, I don't have a choice anyway. The messages announcing the storm resound in my radio. I have to pick up the pace. I quickly move on to the last part. I only need a few more ramps to adjust the direction. Ten seconds later and everything is set. All that's left is to return to the platform I'm using as my launch pad. So far, I've been lucky; no one has noticed my little project. Once I'm at the top, another alert announces that the storm is on the move. In fact, from where I am, I can see the cloud perfectly as it heads my way.

I grip the cart and move toward the ramp. I let the two front wheels touch it. I look out before me and take a deep breath. I'm about to set off, when three shots ring out. The bullets whiz above my head. I turn around and see the young girl from last time standing at the foot of my structure. She puts her weapon away and waves at me. Then she starts emptying a can of spray paint and tags the first section of my project. A rainbow, each end anchored in a fluffy cloud, now adorns my ramp. When I raise my hand to wave back, the cart escapes me and starts its descent. I run toward it, grab it, and push it as hard as I can like a bobsled. After reaching a good speed, I jump on the metal bar supporting the back wheels and lean way forward. I fly faster and faster down the ramp. The metal frame shakes and a terrible sound comes from it. I don't dare look anywhere except at the runway. I'm afraid of the spots where the slope changes. If any of the transitions between the sections are too abrupt, I'll be in deep trouble. In several seconds, I'll know if it works . . . or not.

Yes! It's all good! I want to scream to release the weight of anxiety from my shoulders. Just before it transitions to the horizontal part, I change positions. I move from the front of the vehicle to the back. Boom! Everything goes perfectly; I shoot onto the last part of the ski jump at top speed. Just before arriving at the end, I make myself small, coiling up like a spring and . . . ta-da! At the exact moment the wheels leave the ski jump, I uncoil and stretch upward, but without releasing the bar.

I'm flying! My flight path is perfect. It almost looks like NASA tried to send me into orbit. The wind is whipping my face. The sky

is clear and I can easily see Small Island getting closer. That's it; next I start the downward phase of my flight. In less than twenty seconds, I should hit the grass. The view suddenly makes me smile broadly, almost arrogantly. My heart is racing. Thanks to the pressure of my body at full speed, my lucky vehicle turns into a scrap heap. Together, we slam into a completely invisible barrier that stops us solid. Despite the shock, I stay conscious several seconds, enough time to slide down the transparent wall. I notice it doesn't have a single scratch. Then I land pitifully in the ocean. It was a completely crazy idea. But this is not my last time building structures. In fact, each of my failures gets me a little closer to victory. By eliminating options, I'll end up finding a solution.

The storm. It must be the key to the mystery, so that's how I'll find a way out of here. All my questions revolved around it. From now on, I'll focus entirely on it. Since it travels and shrinks, there must be a system that fuels and moves it. I have good reason to think that it works like the drain in a sink and that everything happens at its center. I have to figure out some things, and the answer is bound to be in the eye of the storm. That's my best option.

This investigation will not be easy. All the participants converge around it. That is where the best contestants go. They face off there once they have done away with the weaklings and defenseless types like me. Before starting this mission impossible, I have to check one last thing.

It took me awhile, but I've finally returned to my favorite location. Away from prying eyes, I can start another substantial collection of raw materials. To clear my mind, I have to bring one last crazy idea to fruition. OK: because of this invisible barrier, any exit by the ocean looks impossible. What about the sky? I have to try it. I'm more efficient at collecting materials now. The storm alerts have already sounded, but that's no problem; I still have some time before the storm gets here. I'm going to construct a ramp that climbs as high as possible into the sky. As long as no one interrupts me, I'll get to see where this leads.

Here we go; I finish destroying things with my pickaxe. I think I have everything I need to reach an amazing height. I take one last look around before starting. I spot the cloud's path and decide to orient my structure in the direction it's traveling. That way, I'll have as much time as possible before being swallowed up by the storm. No one's around . . . Time to get started!

12

THE ANGEL OF DEATH

Before taking off, I turn and look one last time to watch the moving storm. It gives me motivation. My ramp has to take me as high as possible. The goal is to find out if there is anything beyond the clouds. Someone built every inch of this place; I'm sure of it. I feel like I'm locked inside an aquarium or a prison. So I hope that by climbing high enough I'll be able to escape.

I set down the first plank. I take a few steps back to gain momentum and I set off running. Using the right speed, I can run and build simultaneously. As I progress, the planks practically appear at my feet. This is great! The sound of my feet on the wood and of my structure going up is exhilarating. I feel like I've launched a cavalry attack! Unfortunately, the euphoria doesn't last. Less than ten seconds after I start, the first attack against me begins. Why should I keep going? It would be better if I turn back, before it becomes inevitable that I'll fall. This makes me so mad. No one was there. I checked. Where did this person come from? I stop immediately and go back in the other direction. The shots multiply, but I'm not the only target. The shooter himself is being attacked. I seize the opportunity to try to take refuge but then I realize I don't need to because the shots have already stopped.

Perplexed, I scan the surroundings and try to understand what may have just happened. Several dozen yards away is the first pile of weapons and accessories. They must be left over from my aggressor. Farther away, someone emerges from a small two-story tower built for combat. It's HER! She waves, then jumps to the bottom of her structure and finally tags it. Using the same signature: a cluster of small hearts. She continues on with another drawing of a door. As fast as she appeared, she then disappears. What was she saying? I'll think about it later. The storm is right behind me and I have to continue my mission.

So I go back to my crazy ramp construction. As I pass by them, I gather the planks ruined in the attack.

I'm off again running. I quickly get back into the rhythm I'd found. There's no need to look at my feet to make sure my structure is solid, so I keep my gaze focused ahead of me. The higher I get, the more amazing the view. Despite the altitude, I unfortunately see no sign of an exit. I continue climbing, farther and farther, until suddenly I find myself inches from falling into space. No! Fortunately, I have good reflexes. It's impossible to build any higher . . . I'm stuck! What alternative do I have? I notice that I can create horizontal platforms, but as soon as I try to continue my ascent, I fail again. Oh jeez! I feel like a lab rat trapped in a maze, and I'm running low on raw materials. Do I go back and let the storm defeat me? No! So I decide to reverse the slope of my building materials and start to descend. I'll see how far I can go before reaching a dead end. It doesn't take long before I can't build anymore. Even at this height, I sadly can't imagine being able to escape by jumping. So, I watch the storm and notice it has stopped momentarily. This gives me a few minutes of calm. More shots ring out. The starting point of my ramp is still far below me, lost now somewhere in the toxic cloud. Perched in the air, at the end of a wooden ramp shooting into the sky, and with no hills around, who would think to look in my direction? In fact, I bet these bullets are not meant for me. Suddenly, I find myself in the front row watching a battle that just broke out.

The situation looks strange and even unprecedented. At this point, I can only see a single silhouette. He shoots a few rounds. At first, he seems to just run around with no particular purpose. I hear more shots, then realize that this poor soul is simply fleeing. Strangely, his assailant only opens fire on the shelters behind which the "resident" wants to hide. Whether he builds a wall or crouches behind a tree, the result is the same. One or two shots later, he has to run away to find another refuge. It reminds me of the day I found my cat in the yard playing with a mouse. He controlled the situation by letting the mouse think it had a chance to escape . . . The whole thing was sad.

Oh no! When the man being hunted slips and falls, he tries his best to get back on his feet. Moving again, he sets his eyes on the top of the slope he had just fallen down. Almost magically, his hunter is already waiting for him below. He spots him. His prey has not noticed him yet, convinced that the threat is still on the other side.

Seeing him makes my blood freeze. This is someone with a very dark presence. He's wearing crow feathers, or something like that, around his neck. A hood over his head camouflages his facial features. Only his eyes, which look like two small purple marbles floating in oil, glimmer in the dark. The rest of his body is wrapped in leather straps secured with silver buckles. His iron boots and gloves shine with a terrible cold light. The killer is going to swing into action in only a matter of seconds. I have to find a way to create a diversion. Anything will do, but it has to be fast. Rifling quickly through my backpack, I pull out the first object I touch: a first aid kit. Perfect! Without a second thought, I throw it at the poor man who has been trapped.

My throat tightens and it becomes extremely difficult to swallow. The throw I made, which was quite accurate, alerted the young man to my presence. He looks up at me, as does his hunter (whose costume I would love to wear for Halloween). The hunter now completely ignores his prey, to be more precise his "former" prey. My appearance seems to have greatly disturbed the situation. Still staring at me, he pulls the trigger of his sawed-off shotgun. After a terrifying explosion, only two of us remain. I don't know why, but at that exact moment, two things come to mind. First, if he could talk, he would say, "Just the two of us!" Second, it won't be long before I leave my perch, even if it's not in the way I had imagined it.

Curiously, he pauses for a second. Then, with unusual speed and agility, he reaches a height that provides protection while maintaining a totally clear view of me. Even though I'm in his line of fire, I'm almost reassured because at least my sentence will be quick. The first explosion startles me. I hear the bullet whistle by me but it doesn't hit me; it doesn't even graze me.

What's he doing? I can't believe a monster like him would miss his target unless he's just trying to intimidate me. There's no need to waste his ammunition; his presence alone strikes me with terror . . .

Out of the blue, he makes a friendly gesture toward me, a "hello" that clearly is meant to mean "good-bye." Then he shoots one more time. His bullet has the same effect as the last one. To my surprise, I'm still standing. I have just enough time to see him turn on his heels and disappear instantly. I don't know if it's my emotions, but I feel a slight trembling. I extend my arm to check and see that my hand is perfectly still. I'm still in complete control of my body. At this point, I hear the sound of dominoes falling, and I realize he destroyed the base of my ramp and it's starting to crumble. What a mess! Undoubtedly the work of a madman. I'll most likely disappear when my construction does. However, I plan to leave with dignity. I tilt my head back and set my eyes on the horizon. It's almost poetic . . .

Here we go. I fall toward the ground, along with the rest of my ramp. I barely have time to glance beneath my feet before explosions sound. I notice that someone started creating a tower to save me. As I fall, the building's stories pile on top of each other. But the Good Samaritan's projects are under attack by revolvers and automatic weapons.

It's impossible for me to tell who's shooting who, but I do know one thing: I'm still around to talk about it. The combat that has been unleashed is like a hurricane destroying everything in its path. The elements built by this battle's participants, simultaneously appear, and then disappear almost as quickly.

They create a swirling movement that rises and falls. The question is, who will manage to box the other in? I never would have imagined you could build structures for that purpose. It's amazing! I'm completely enthralled with this turn of events. My best move is to run like crazy. They don't need my help to settle their score.

I don't really know which path to take to get back to solid ground without being spotted. The shortest path between two points is a straight line! I jump on the wooden planks left standing after the rain of bullets. Suddenly my heart stops! In front of me, two glowing purple marbles gaze at me. A half-second later, the man in black has disappeared and I find myself trapped inside a wooden cube. My anxiety level increases because of all the weapons firing, plus the sounds of running and jumping. At this low point, I suddenly recognize a sound. A commotion echoes inside my prison, mixed with sounds of springs and metal plates. This means that, in the midst of this frenzy, mechanical traps have started to appear. Get near one and huge spikes will spring up and impale you. The image that comes to mind is a rattlesnake striking at its prey. Worst of all, they can be set inside the floor or the ceiling. The walls could be covered in them, too. The situation couldn't get any worse.

Before making another move, I try to look through the planks. I want to be able to see where they have been placed. What I see has nothing to do with the traps: it's HER again! My protector is a girl. I grab my pickaxe to break down the wall separating us. When I finish destroying it, she has already disappeared. If I think about the origin of the explosions, it means she must have taken the stairway in front of me. I take off after her, but I have barely reached the first steps when a blast slashes the boards under my feet. I have to turn back and find another route. But I can't leave her alone with this psychopath. Despite the shots, I keep climbing. When I finally reach an area where I can spot the shooter, it's already too late. I have just enough time to see the gentle, apologetic gaze of my savior who, despite her best efforts, did not manage to dissuade me from taking the stairs. The last thing I hear is the click of the trap that my feet just triggered: I'm done for.

13

SIGN LANGUAGE

I've seen people escape the traps used here. It requires great speed and Olympic form. However, I don't have fast enough reflexes to dodge them yet. When a click tells me that I've triggered one, my first reflex is to cower and cover my head. Unfortunately, when one is coming at breakneck speed toward me, this does me no good. Once again, my encounter did not have a happy ending. Despite that, I'm still very happy to see her. She is still the only person who has shown me any compassion. She has extended her hand to me every time the opportunity has arose. I know nothing about her or her motivations . . . Even her first name is a mystery. I've never believed in fate. But this kind of experience could easily convince me that luck is not the only thing driving this vehicle.

As we get older, we learn to see the big picture. I've always feared the unknown. To reassure myself, I've always established bases to support my world. Places where I knew I wasn't in any danger, where I was safe. When I was little, I took refuge under my bed. It became my fortress, the walled castle where I could hide. Then, I included my closet, my bedroom, and the entire house.

I expanded my territory by setting up tiny bases everywhere: in my best friend's room, at the comic book store, or on the park bench by the large fountain near school. To shake off a harsh or tough situation, I would just take refuge in one of those spots. Once there, I immediately felt relief as well as a sense of safety.

Today, I realize that I've reproduced this pattern on Big Island. I've become attached to certain locations. I land there systematically. No matter what direction the flying bus takes, I choose a designated drop-off point, a location I know by heart, where I repeat a well-established routine. This way, I can constantly reproduce the same acts at my own pace. Over time, I start to feel at home. These places belong to me and they reassure me. Thanks to them, I can calmly keep studying how the storm works. They offer me a great starting point to set out and conquer its center.

Since my terrifying encounter with the man in black, a real Angel of Death, something strange has happened. Every time I set out on Big Island, all of my landmarks are now tagged with the same signature. I would know it anywhere. Before each journey, she now takes the time to notice my landing point and leaves me a small mark there. I must admit that I'm never the first to leave the bus or the first to touch down. That gives her plenty of time to work before I arrive. The moments before I jump are important for my well-being and mental health. They keep me away from the inevitable stress involved in my quest for freedom. I can tell you that the expression "the calm before the storm" means more to me than it does to a sailor on the ocean . . .

It's more than a simple "hello." She's setting the stage for me. She clears the area as well as she can before my landing. I don't know her goal, but I know it includes me. In a place like this, having a scout, a guardian angel, is a luxury that can't be refused. Thanks to her, I can double or even triple my exploration time. I sense that I'm very close to arriving at the center of the storm. I just have to persevere.

Today, I don't know why, is unlike any other. It's "backward day." Nothing goes according to plan. It's the worst! Everything seems backward. At times like this, I become my own worst enemy. I messed up my exit from the bus and as a result, I'm going to land earlier than planned. I hate when my routine is off; it stresses me out. So I try to get things back to normal. I shouldn't listen to myself; I should trust myself. Why do I want to rush everything? I have to take my time. What if, this time, I follow the river to escape the storm? I could cut through the mountains . . .

I land behind a house at the southern tip of Big Island. It offers many advantages. Located along a cliff, away from everything, it reminds me of an entrenched fort. To top it off, it overlooks the area. Once inside, it will be impossible to take me by surprise. Also, it often contains a chest in the attic. That is one of the benefits of knowing how to build: everything becomes accessible. Despite my own hesitations, as soon as I touch down I run and take refuge in the house. But, before reaching it, I find myself face to face with an intruder. Panic strikes; I prepare to scurry away like a rabbit. Then, I realize she is standing calmly in front of me. My arrival did not cause her any concern. She reacts nonchalantly, as if we had planned to meet.

After a few awkward seconds, I use my pickaxe to tap on the ground the only Morse code I know: three short taps, three long taps, three short taps: SOS. Why did I do that? That's stupid! Miserable backward day! I didn't take the time to think: if she doesn't know Morse code, she'll think I'm crazy since there is no imminent danger. What's worse! She could respond with a message I don't know how to decode . . .

The first alerts sound, predicting the storm's arrival. Their loud sound surprises me. Then I realize that of course she gets the same messages as I do, at the same time. While they stress me out a little, she doesn't seem at all affected by them.

She looks at me and pulls out her spray paint. She draws a winners' podium, then an arrow pointing at the first place spot. Next, she looks up at me and points to the top step. I follow her direction and go stand where she indicated. She does a little victory dance. Unfortunately I have no idea what she is trying to tell me. That's when she pulls her weapon out of her backpack and tries to give it to me. I take offense and turn down her offer. Then she draws a question mark. I give her a small wave, telling her to be patient. Next, I try to explain to her what I'm doing.

Like we're playing charades, I lift my index finger to indicate there is one word. Next, I point in her direction and stand like a strong man. I strut over to stand opposite my previous location. With one hand, I simulate holding a camera. With the other, I move my hand like I'm turning a crank, to simulate recording. She bursts out laughing and starts clapping. I hesitate to laugh with her, even though, deep down, I can relate. She notices right away and tosses me her spray paint.

I write my first name on the ground and toss the can back to her. Next to mine, she writes "Ella." I smile and reach out to shake her hand. Ella is a very pretty name. In response, she grabs a semi-automatic weapon and bullets fly. An assailant had appeared behind me and she saved my life again. She gestures, saying we need to move because the shots could attract more people. Plus, the storm will arrive soon. To my disappointment, it's too late to get to know each other better. We set out toward the north. She spends most of her time jumping and flipping, and yet she moves faster than me. I think it's her technique to spot suspicious movements around her. However, if I tried that, it would make me barf.

After following a ridge, we start to climb up a hill. We finally reach a large factory with a smoke stack extending high into the sky. These buildings have obviously served as battlegrounds many times, as is apparent by the scattered remains of wooden structures. One loud shot rings out. The projectile explodes less than one yard away from me. One and then two rounds of bullets hit me directly. Without knowing how, I find myself inside a stone box. At my feet, Ella lays down several bandages and a deep blue potion. Simultaneously, she creates an opening in the back wall of my new shelter, then exits and shuts it immediately before disappearing.

I bandage myself up as best I can, then consider the strange drink. What could it be? Is this a cool mint drink? I open it to sniff the contents. I know that's not very polite, but who's going to

give me grief here, within these four stone walls? It has no smell.
I decide to down the entire contents. Incapable of appreciating
the taste, I definitely feel refreshed after drinking that strange
liquid. If I ever find one of those potions, I'll keep it in my
backpack with the rest of my equipment. It just might come in
handy.

I raise my pickaxe and create an exit. How long was I in there?
I don't hear any more shots. When I stick my head out, I see
the storm arriving. I pause; should I go around the factory? Cut
through the buildings? Today, I know that, above all, I should not
follow my instincts because it's a backward day. Not much time
is left. I go straight into the lion's den. I cross my fingers that my
guardian angel is still in the area. I set out down the center lane,
where weapons are scattered on the ground, and continue on
my path. I glance about, hoping to spot her. The farther I get, the
more concerned I become. Her disappearance is not a good sign.
When I reach the last building, I can't keep myself from stopping.
The open door really makes me want to go in and poke around. I
look back to gauge the cloud's location.

Thirty seconds; I won't need more than that to check it out.
Who knows? Maybe she needs my help? After everything she's
done for me, am I just going to continue selfishly on my way? No,
I can't do that.

I disappear inside the first room, only to find nothing out of
the ordinary. I go through two adjoining rooms without wasting
time. My stress level increases. Completely torn between guilt
and pride, I get myself together and enter the offices. I look all

over, terrified of finding her hurt in a corner somewhere but there's nothing.

As I'm about to turn around and leave, I notice the bathrooms. What better place to hide than this private place? I have to hurry because I already hear the storm rumbling. I hurry inside. The floor is covered with all kinds of accessories, weapons, and materials. In my rush, I can't stop myself in time. My brain does make the connection between all these objects and the closed door. Backward day comes to an end thanks to a perfectly placed trap.

14

EVERYONE WINS

In the TV studio, around a hundred people clap to the wild beat of techno music. Frantically, a host dances like it's the last day of summer vacation. With a wave, he makes the music, clapping, and choreography stop in less than one second.

"Hey! Hey! Hey! We know how to bring the house down! Don't we, guys? Tonight is extra special. Our guest is a genius. I love this guy. Mark Langelo! He's the mind behind . . ."

Then, he turns toward his audience. He shouts, "*Battle for,*" and they yell back, "*Domination!.*" After the third time, he barely moves his hand and silence fills the studio.

"Mark, they love you . . . And let me say, you've clearly earned it; your show is my favorite! When I'm watching it, no one can talk to me; I'm totally addicted. It's fantastic! We'll talk about it in a few seconds with your crew because there are some big controversies around your show. I recommend you stay till the end because we have a huge surprise for you! Justine Lexael, our journalist who always takes on the tough assignments, participated in the filming of a scene in the next Jane Doe movie. You don't want to miss it! You'll see; it's completely wild! Now for a short break and, afterward, we'll be back with Mark Langelo and his crew."

After a short commercial, the host, dancing on the stage again, abruptly silences the room with another wave. He picks up where he left off,

"Now, where was I? Hey, Mark! In your game, as terrible as I would have been at eliminating the others, I would have rocked everyone with my dancing!"

The audience applauds. A reporter interrupts.

"I'm sorry, but I think this game is unhealthy . . ."

The host immediately takes back his role as the head of the show.

"Frances Delarive, what did you say?"

"I said that mixing things together is never good . . ."

More participants join in the discussion.

"Frances is right . . ."

"No! It's not a big deal, it's just a game! Relax a little!"

The host attempts to regain control of his show.

"No! No! No! Not all at once. We can't understand you when you all talk at the same time . . . Christian Abelle is right; it's just a game!"

Frances speaks up again.

"It's a bad example for our youth, that much is clear. If you combine violence and . . ."

The host interrupts Frances to make the audience laugh.

"But your hairstyle, you think that's a good example for young people? Mark, Mark . . . What do you think about the controversy around your game?"

"We spent years creating and developing this concept. We consulted the top specialists, doctors, and psychologists. Just look at the audience polls to see that we did a great job."

"You're right, Mark, it can't be denied. The numbers say a lot."

"If I may . . ."

"Of course, Mark, make yourself at home!"

"My game represents the school of life. We all learn from life. We all know how it can make you happy, then one second later, it all gets taken away and you don't even see it coming."

Speaking to the audience and reporters directly, he adds, "I think everyone agrees on that, right? When you fall down, what do you do? Do you stay there? No! Of course not! You find the strength to get back up, get back in the saddle, and start again. That is the example I want to give our youth. Those are the values we're fighting for. That's what our game is!"

The entire room starts clapping. The host takes over again.

"Frances . . . Mark is right, that's how life is. Just open a newspaper or watch the news. It's full of good and bad stories. One minute, you're laughing. The next, you're crying! And to make myself feel better, I don't know about you, but I like to . . . dance!"

Music starts playing and the host does a ridiculous dance. Then, with a wave, he stops everything again. He continues on as if nothing happened. Like a student, a reporter raises his hand.

"Ladies and gentlemen, this is a big moment on the show. Kevin Kervideck wants to say something!"

"Well, the game is, after all . . . You have to kill everyone!
Those are great values . . ."

Mark pretends to faint.

"Dear sweet Kevin! Do you want me to die? I almost had
a heart attack! I think you are one of the only people here
who's never watched my show. Not a single one of the one
hundred contestants has died or is going to die. It's actually
quite the opposite! They're all in great shape! Right now, they're
surrounded by a team of fantastic doctors in a center with the
most modern technology, where nothing can happen to them.
I promise you that they're receiving better medical care than
anyone else on Earth. Even better than the president of the
United States! The worst that can happen is that they leave the
game richer than any of us will ever be."

"Now, don't twist my words. You know what I mean. Dead
or not, it's the slogan 'there can be only one' that I don't like.
You have to destroy everyone else to win, and you even do that
without facing any consequences. We're sick of the self-interest
that lies around every corner in this society."

"Mr. Kervideck doesn't speak very often, but when he does
open his mouth, he doesn't mince words! Mark? Does Kevin have
a point?"

"I think he's mistaken."

After flashing the host a big smile, Mark addresses Kevin.

"Our game is a metaphor for life. It has nothing to do with
self-interest."

"'Our game is a metaphor for life.' That's great! Mark, you should get that printed on T-shirts and you'll become a millionaire!"

"Good thing you said millionaire, because our contestants can BECOME millionaires. And believe me, it takes more than just checking a few boxes on a piece of paper to win the jackpot. In our game, you have to fight, you have to overcome. If you do your best, you will be compensated. If you don't bring your A-game, you'll pay for your mistakes right away! Those are the values we're defending, and that's the real deal!"

"That's great! I think it's beautiful! A round of applause for Mark!"

The host encourages the audience to stand and applaud the producer. The two men, clearly satisfied with themselves, flash each other a knowing look. The host continues.

"I have an idea! We didn't plan it, but we could conduct a small survey, right here, just us. At home, pick up your phone and tell us what you think of *Battle for Domination*. This show is yours, too! In the meantime, we'll take a short break and be right back."

After the commercial ends, everyone onstage is dancing. The host is getting down, too. Then, with a wave of his hand, everyone stops dancing and pays attention.

"We're back. Tonight, the person winning more than the others is Mark Langelo! The creator of *Battle for Domination*! Let's give Mark a round of applause!"

The audience obeys. With a wry smile, Mark bows his head as a sign of appreciation.

"You deserve it, Mark. You revolutionized TV game shows; you pushed the limits further than anyone before you. Bravo. Anyway, that's my opinion. What do the viewers at home think? It's time to look at our survey."

On the giant studio screen a question is displayed: "For or against *Battle for Domination?*" Just below, the gauge showing the supportive votes shoots up to ninety percent. The boisterous host speaks up,

"Mark, that's a dictator's score right there! But it's really not surprising since your show is taking off. Not only here, but all over the world."

"We win worldwide during every prime time episode."

"WORLDWIDE, my friends! That's amazing!"

"We really count on all the social media networks. Our live show rebroadcasts on lots of media platforms. Our number one priority is to make sure that everyone can watch and everyone can participate, no matter what country they're watching in."

"That's genius! I'll tell you, I always vote for the Angel of Death. He terrifies and fascinates me. He seems to be invincible!! Which player is your favorite?"

The Angel of Death ends up winning the majority at the table. However, it's impossible to say for sure if the reporters being asked even know what they're talking about. It seems like their answers were just attempts to impress the host. Then Frances casts her vote.

"I like the young woman who is doing well right now."

Mark takes the bait put out for him.

"I'd like to take this opportunity to say that we were careful to choose our contestants in terms of equality. Girls are just as capable as boys of exceptional performances, and Ella is the best proof of that."

Kevin suddenly speaks up.

"There are rumors that an anti-gun activist has infiltrated the show's contestants . . ."

The host tries to defuse the situation as quickly as possible.

"Wow, Mr. Kervideck really is on it today! Be a good sport, Kevin; just because Mark blew you out of the water earlier doesn't mean you can spread rumors dug out of the garbage can."

Calmly, Mark prepares his response.

"We are very proud of our game, our choice of contestants, and the way things are going right now. No one has done what we have before. However it's normal that, with such success, we would make some people jealous. You know what they say about sticks and stones? They break your bones, but words never hurt anyone . . . As for the contestant you're alluding to, he's developing his own strategy. Our game brings out everyone's personality. Some are born fighters; others, like him, are diehards who think they can take advantage of the others' failures and win. At the risk of repeating myself, our game is no more or less than a metaphor for life. You can't have a coin with just one side. If you do, that means you're a cheater. And cheating is not our policy. We support the truth! And the audience knows that; otherwise they wouldn't watch it every day like they do. We don't like cheaters! We are interested in winners. But, since every coin has two sides, losers come with the winners!"

"I don't know about you all, but personally, Mark, you've convinced me; I won't say any more. You've won me over!"

The host starts applauding, and the reporters and audience quickly do the same.

"We'll be right back after another break for Justine Lexael's report from the day she spent backstage filming the show. Don't move. We'll be right back!"

15

EVERYTHING MAKES SENSE

I head toward one of my usual starting points. My thoughts are focused on Ella. It was great interacting with another human without it involving shooting at each other! I had almost forgotten how gratifying it can be to feel like you're more than prey to someone. I would have loved to understand her drawing better. Why draw a winner's podium? It's only a matter of time before I figure it out. The next time we see each other, I'll try to be better. From now on, I can count on my new ally who surely will give me some much-needed help. In fact, all my theories have been proven wrong so far. All the leads I've followed have only led me to dead ends. I couldn't find the exit or start of a supply route. I haven't found any clues to help me find the machine operating this awful storm. My only hope lies in one person now: Ella.

During short encounters, I know we'll manage to communicate using her spray paint. I keep using my regular drop-off points because she knows them, too. From now on, I'll jump from the bus as soon as possible so I can meet up with her quicker.

I land in one of the houses located on a cliff and head directly for the basement. I start to remove everything with my pickaxe. My goal is to clear off the walls and floor so we can write on them easily. I'm not concerned about the noise. Since I've been visiting this area, I've learned there's nothing to be afraid of here. I'm anxious to see her and cleaning the basement is a great distraction. About twenty seconds after starting, I suddenly think I hear an echo. I turn and there she is; she started destroying the room, too. A wave of joy washes over me. Strangely, I feel the same nervousness that accompanies a first kiss. However, neither of us dares make such a move. She stops and turns toward me. We greet each other with a wave. She nods toward the remaining materials to be collected. I feel like one of the seven dwarfs: I'm working in the mine with Snow White and it's kind of fun.

We quickly finish our task. Then she tosses the spray paint at my feet. I use it to draw on the wall I just cleared. Hastily, I sketch an open-mouthed smiley face. I pose like a bad boy to make her laugh, then immediately bow toward her. Like a comedian going onstage, I want to show her I can laugh at myself. Her only response is to perform the same movement. That's how our unique form of communication begins. Like two rappers, we start a sort of battle. Only instead of passing a microphone back and forth, it's a can of spray paint. I get the ball rolling.

"What's this place?? Are we dead??"

Surprised, Ella flashes me a smile that covers, for better or worse, a laugh. Then, she writes, "We're in the game, of course!"

"What game? I'm here to be in a movie."

"*Battle for Domination.*"

"I thought that was the code name for the movie . . ."

"What movie?"

This time, I don't catch the spray paint in the air. It falls on the ground and rolls to my feet. Where am I? In a game? What kind of game? I've only seen people dancing and shooting each other . . . While I'm thinking, Ella approaches me and picks up the can. With a gesture of goodwill, she reassures me and signals that everything is fine. I show her my appreciation with a very sincere smile. I restart our communication, continuing on another wall.

"How do we get out?"

"You have to be Number 1."

"Number 1?"

"You have to beat everyone. The last one standing wins the right to leave or stay in the game."

Then it hits me hard. I don't stand a chance of getting out. I'm completely and utterly doomed. She winks at me and continues.

"I'll help you get out."

"That's impossible. I refuse to shoot at anyone."

"I'll teach you . . ."

"No way! No weapons for me."

"Why not? You don't have a choice if you want out!"

Her way of insisting triggers so much emotion in me that I can't contain it. My eyes burn. I'm sure they're red. I turn away and pretend to sniffle to convince her I'm about to sneeze. She slowly comes closer and puts her hand on my shoulder. I take a step back and, without looking at her, I signal to her that everything is fine and this will blow over. A tear rolls down my cheek. I breathe in deep and turn and write on the wall:

"I'll help you get out."

She rolls her eyes upward. I continue and tap the wall with my hand.

"You get out."

"And then?"

"Explain to them there was a mistake."

"They won't believe me."

"I've never used a weapon once in here."

I feel like I'm starting to convince her. I take her arm and look into her eyes. She nods her head in agreement. Then, she writes, "We need a strategy to do this right."

"Anything you want."

"Anything?"

"No weapons, though. I won't touch those deadly things."

The alerts sound, announcing the arrival of another storm. We have to get moving.

Once outside, a quick glance at the sky is enough to get my bearings. I now know from experience which direction I need to go. I know another house, farther along, where we can continue our conversation. I point in the direction of the building. She agrees, and we set out along the north coast. The terrain offers us a natural cover that protects us.

Arriving at the beat-up cabin, we hear the creak of a trunk. Before I have time to propose a plan, Ella is already on the roof, pickaxe in hand, and creating an entrance directly to our treasure. In less than ten seconds, she forces it open, then comes back out with another weapon and ammunition. She has a strange smile on her lips. Then she hands me an unusual object. I accept her gift, but not without a little apprehension. I can't tell whether it's a joke, a poisoned gift, or something that could actually be useful.

Entirely synthetic and covered in plastic leaves, the thing looks just like actual greenery. She gestures for me to put it on. Oh wow, this is great! It turns out that she found a suit, but not just any suit: a "camouflaged shrubbery" costume. It sounds absolutely ridiculous, but once I have it on, I bet it will be really useful. I put it on immediately. I would love to have a mirror to see what it looks like. I can only imagine how I look, but it fits me perfectly. Overjoyed, I throw myself at Ella and hug her, my way of saying thank you.

Unfortunately, my movements take me aback a little. They cause the costume to produce a strange sound, like you'd hear if you were wearing a rain coat or a wetsuit. Well, that's what it felt like at that point. Oh well, we'll see . . . I'm ready to test my luck. Nothing ventured, nothing gained. I take a few steps, then crouch down in the grass. Ella approves of the result.

In this position, I'm completely undetectable. Also, I still have an excellent view of the exterior. It's perfect for me.

In the distance, an explosion sounds. At the same time, a bullet whistles by our ears. A sniper has spotted us. Ella signals for me to continue on to the next house, then rushes away to take care of the isolated shooter. Now is not the time for negotiating. I do what she wants without protest. We split up and go in different directions.

A few minutes later, I reach the top of a hill. At the summit, there are several bizarrely arranged stones. They almost seem to resemble Stonehenge. Hiding behind one of them, I quickly assess the situation. A little farther along and below are a barn and the house where we're supposed to meet up again. They're far enough away to escape the storm, but also close enough that I can get to them without running much risk. Based on past experience, I now understand the more time that passes, the smaller the safe zone becomes, and then bad things start to happen.

Given the choice between a house in good condition and a rundown barn, anyone would clearly choose the more comfortable of the two. It's only logical. Without a second thought, I rush toward the completely ruined structure. I'll be safer there while I wait for Ella. Everything goes according to plan . . . well, almost. I do, in fact, escape the storm and avoid any bad encounters. However, in my rush to get inside, I don't see the pile of tires. They're the same as the ones on the training course on Small Island. Before I have time to do anything, they launch me up into the air, as if I've just jumped on a trampoline. The noise my ejection makes is comical, but the situation is not. I hit the ceiling of the barn and find myself stuck upstairs. Panicking, I try to fall back down to the first floor so I can hide behind a box or something like that. Not again! I fall back onto the tires and they send me right back where I came from. A cloud of synthetic leaves from my costume fills the air with each sudden movement. I give up. Well, I'd like to, because at the moment,

I'm still stuck upstairs. The idea of using my situation to catch my breath crosses my mind, but the roof is full of holes. If a passerby looks up, he would see a weird guy stuck in the building's crossbeams.

This time, I do my best to jump down to a better place. It's too late! I hear a creak from the house. Stuck like a stake in the door frame, I only have a second to decide what to do. There's a huge wooden box at the back of the barn with enough space to hide behind. However, if someone decides to look around, I would stick out like a sore thumb in this bush costume. The only other option is to hide in the grass. With a rustle of plastic foliage, I throw myself outside, along the outer wall. I try to stick to one of the angles formed by the walls to maintain maximum visibility.

Before I can do that, though, the barn floor creaks under the weight of the stranger who just left the house. I'm sure he heard me. He pauses. Obviously, I don't move an inch. The spot where I'm standing completely still unfortunately doesn't offer a good view since it's behind the building. He shoots a round of shots. Followed by three fast explosions. Then he continues with three more shots spaced apart. The bullets go in all directions, bouncing off the wooden debris, which splinters everywhere. Another round of three fast shots is followed by silence. I would know that sound anywhere; it's the only Morse code I know: SOS! It must be Ella . . . She's making sure that I was the one behind all the racket.

I take the risk of running into the stranger. Once inside the barn, I don't see anyone. Then the moment I turn to rush out of there, I feel a presence that startles me. Ella grabs me without a sound.

How I wish I could yell at her right now! Laughing hysterically, she clearly seems very pleased with her joke. Completely annoyed, I set out toward the house.

Once inside, I don't feel well. I know we have to find an effective strategy together to make this work. However before that, I have to get a weight off my shoulders. I grab the spray paint and sketch a goofy child shooting at jars of jam. I signal that it's me. Then, behind the targets, I add a cat, laying on its side.

I lower my head to pretend I'm crying. I hope she will understand. No one and nothing can give it back. Even though it was just an accident, there's no changing what happened. After that, I swore that I would never touch a gun again.

When I lift my head, our gazes cross. I can see that my story touched her. She comes over to me and hugs me. I don't know where all this is leading us, but I know now that I have a true friend.

16

VOYAGE TO THE CENTER OF THE WAR

Mark Langelo strides into the control room for the game *Battle for Domination*. He yells at one of the employees, "This could really be serious!"

It doesn't startle the employee. He doesn't even bother to turn his head and establish visual contact. His eyes stay glued to his computer screen. With the mouse, he rewinds the video to a specific moment. Mark violently hits the desk and leans forward to watch. There, he sees Ella and Paul's interaction. No reaction shows on his face, and nothing comes out of his mouth. He maintains an uncanny calm, which is a bad omen, while the video continues to play.

"OK, set that video aside for me just in case . . . I'll do what I have to do."

He leaves the room, repeating a strange expression that no one can hear.

"The wimp is a bird fallen from its nest."

He goes back to his office and calls his lawyer.

"Legally, can you promise me that we're covered? We have his signature on several documents . . . And the simple argument

'I didn't know what I was doing' won't hold up. Except in the case of dementia, or something like that, after getting a medical opinion . . . Yes, in other words, nothing will happen. Everything's OK; we have no reason to worry. The boy will leave at the end of the season with the others. We won't talk about him. He's just a kid like the others, period."

He hangs up the phone, his mood lightened. He glances at his watch and then leaves the room without wasting time.

In the meantime, on Big Island . . .

After comforting me, Ella decides to take me into the adjacent room to prepare our plan of attack. We can't drag our feet; time is running out. This time, we're not clearing the room; it's more narrow. Also, the location has already had visitors, which reduces the chances of a bad encounter considerably, especially if we don't attract any attention. There's still plenty left to do to plan our exit.

With a series of sketches, she explains our strategy. To summarize, we have to figure out what kinds of enemies we're facing. To fight them, we need short, long, and medium-range weapons.

An attacker jumps on his prey? Keep him at a distance and slow his efforts by creating structures and walls, weakening him little by little.

A sniper camps out at our location? Hide and wait for him to recharge, then attack him head-on.

There's a major advantage to working as a pair in a world where everyone is only out for himself. So, I act like a pack horse, carrying the potions and first aid. And Ella, relieved of the accessories, has enough room in her inventory to carry all kinds of weapons, which the others can't do. On the other hand, our strength is where our Achilles heel lies. When we're separated, we become especially vulnerable. We'll move along like a caterpillar: in a wave. She'll lead the way, stopping every ten yards. If the path is clear, I just have to join her. We create several commands using a very rudimentary code based on hand signals. Without making a sound, we can give orders like "hide," "go forward," "don't move," "danger," "it's clear," or even "I need help." The one I like the least is "bait." In a crisis, I have to create a diversion, giving Ella the time to get the upper hand. Last thing: for our strategy to work, we have to stay very close to the storm. It must always be behind us. If a battle forces us to stay in our positions too long, we'll run the risk of getting sandwiched in and stuck there. It's not the perfect strategy, but I think it puts luck on our side. We're ready to take first place on the podium.

While we prepare to leave the house, Ella suddenly grabs my arm, keeping me from opening the door. There seems to be a commotion taking place outside. When I hear confusion like that, I head instinctively to the window to look. Ella and I watch a big battle between a guy hiding behind a tree and a builder. The builder has made two or three wooden fences to protect himself. It feels like I'm watching a real show. Ella shoves me hard, causing me to realize that in less than a second, I've already forgotten all the rules we just established. With a quick wink, she breaks the tension between us. Then she gives me the signal meaning, "Hide until the next command!" I immediately obey. Well, halfway. I can't help it (maybe, in another life, I was a guard), I have to raise my head to watch the two combatants through the window. An irrational desire drives me to watch these spectacular events unfold, even though they're not that exciting.

Ella has gone out the back door and climbed up the house. Once she's on the roof, the sound of her footsteps indicates her position. I'd bet the two combatants haven't heard a thing. A tree tips over, under someone's deafening shots, requiring the other to find a better refuge. Full of panic, he heads toward our shelter. No! No! No! I can't let him in. I can't take that risk.

Then an idea comes to me! Whether it's a stroke of genius or colossal mistake, only time will tell. The best defense is to attack, so I rush to the door and open it to surprise the man fleeing toward us. Upon seeing me, he's startled, then disappears instantly, under the shots from his adversary and Ella.

I don't know why, but suddenly a shiver runs down my spine. Like I'm standing by a draft, even though I realize the air has nothing to do with it. Next, as if out of nowhere, the man in black appears behind his retreating adversary. Absorbed in combat, we didn't see or hear him coming. I'm now convinced he is, in fact, an Angel of Death.

What's he doing here? He seems to have a sixth sense that lets him detect fear. I'm sure he's capable of smelling sweat from miles away, like a shark smells blood. There's no doubt that the

destroyer will take out this entire part of the map in no time, the three of us included. With a pump-action shotgun, he takes a shot at his closest enemy. He doesn't have time to finish him, because Ella has already started peppering him with bullets from her automatic weapon.

Everything happens so fast that I don't even think about going back inside to take shelter. The Angel of Death builds two metal walls opposite us, which gives him the time to take down his first prey. He knows that his protection is solid enough that Ella is just wasting ammunition. He has also determined that, by the time she reaches him, he will have finished with the other competitor. That way, he will be able to have a big welcome waiting for her. I hear a trap spring into action. I realize that only three of us remain: the Angel of Death, Ella, and me. The fury of combat ends as quickly as it started and leaves only a deathly silence. I can't see my protector. I'm sure she is holed up in a tower that she built on top of the house. Her priority is to do everything possible to prevent him from getting closer to us. In the meantime, he must be trying to catch his breath.

This fake calm makes me realize that I'm still out in the open. I immediately go back inside to take refuge. Without thinking, I slam the door, then glue myself to the window to watch the terrible combat that is about to ensue. Attracted by the sound, our nemesis leaves his shelter to look around. What follows next is the loudest explosion possible on the islands: that of the strongest sniper rifle. It's capable of destroying wood and stone walls in one blast. It could kill a dinosaur with a single bullet. Hit hard, the Angel of Death doubles over. Ella takes advantage and turns the pressure up by shooting wildly in his direction. When she finally stops, the sound of a mechanical trampoline resonates. Our enemy has decided to retreat. He knows Ella; he knows it's too dangerous to battle her when he is badly injured. The sniper is near the center of the storm. He has decided to leave and find refuge somewhere to get his energy back and take revenge on the girl who shot him in the back. This way, he'll be in a good place to wait to kill us.

After about thirty seconds, I finally let my shoulders relax. Like at a dentist's office, I had tensed up all of my muscles under the pressure of stress without realizing it. I feel like I'm relaxing a bit; Ella startles me again when she comes in the back door, a smile on her face. She gives me a signal to ask if I'm doing OK, if I was hurt. I stand up, go over to her, and start to turn in a circle to show her that I made it without a scratch. My legs start to wobble, and I almost fall down. She smiles, then quickly looks out the windows. Once she feels we're safe, she inspects each weapon and reloads them. The storm is approaching and it's essential that we move faster. Before leaving the house, she turns toward me and makes a gesture that we didn't prepare, but I know exactly what it means: "Perfect!"

17

FALLING FROM HIGH

Here, there are no easy battles, only victory or defeat. Either you continue, give up, or start over. We are determined and we'll make it, no matter what happens. There's no question that the path we're on will lead us to victory. Forced to run from the awful storm, Ella and I leave the house. We start advancing as planned, like a caterpillar. We respect each other's role: she's the scout, staying ahead of me to detect enemies and clean up if necessary; I'm the troubled soul who, once the danger is gone, joins his heroine. I'm fascinated by the intelligence and effectiveness of her movements: she takes the terrain into account, uses natural obstacles to her advantage, and increases her jumps and changes direction to ward off potentially hidden shooters.

Suddenly, she notices an enemy and immediately builds a ramp directed at the threat. She covers it with three walls: one in front, one on the right, and one on the left. The idea is to get up high, while remaining as protected as possible so she can observe her enemy's reaction. She shoots first. Several seconds later, the retaliation sounds. Ella doesn't leave her perch though or add anything to her structure. Crouched down, she simply performs short, lateral movements between which she stands, shoots, and then returns to cover. She also takes the time to reload her weapons.

I feel like I'm watching a dance. Unfortunately, the performance is ruined by a round of shots from my right. One of them hits me hard. I build the best wooden wall I can between the shooter and me. The sound did not escape Ella. I'm her priority and she'll come help as soon as possible.

I try to distance myself from the attacker. She arrives and I hear her building something. Everywhere I look, I see only wooden boards. My wall finally falls under the shots, and my enemy heads toward me, gun in hand. At the same time, Ella appears from above on a ramp, leaping toward my attacker. While she's still in the air, she puts away her automatic rifle and grabs a pump-action shotgun. Then she unloads it on him before touching the ground. All around her appear blue potions, first aid kits, and a good arsenal.

To my surprise, instead of sorting through the objects, she turns around and hurries toward me. I try to show her my appreciation, but I find myself surrounded by walls and a ceiling. The moment the new structure forms, shots ring out. Ella's first enemy has followed her, requiring her to fight. She has saved me two times in less than thirty seconds, protecting me while also risking her life. Outside, there's no sound. A door appears in one of the walls. It opens and Ella appears, then goes in and shuts it behind her.

She's tense, still full of adrenaline from fighting. She has been seriously hit this time. I open my first aid kits and lay them out for her. She thanks me and bandages herself in the aftermath of the battle. Side by side, we stand up. Before starting our trip again, she asks how I'm feeling with a nod. I give her two thumbs up and an exaggerated wink. I try to let her know that I'm fine, that I'm cool, even though it isn't true.

After the usual precautions, she exits the box we were hiding in and points the way, and we set out again. As we leave, I pick up all the objects left by our previous enemies. Ella gathers the ammunition.

Following the geography of the land, we progress in sections of about ten yards at a time. This time, we run into an obstacle. We arrive at a plain so open and unobstructed that we can't both cross it simultaneously. She signals for me to stay down until she reaches a pile of boulders much farther away. No problem. I squat down and construct a small stone structure with a top—kind of like a giant hat—under which I'll be safe. She approves of my choice and, like a rabbit, bounds off across the field. She makes sure that nothing will catch her by surprise.

While she puts distance between us, I notice a bush moving on the prairie to her right. I'm not the only one who likes this camouflage suit. On the other hand, not realizing I'm there, it's imitating Ella's movements. That can't be an accident. I think he noticed her and is planning to wait until she stops, then shoot at her with a sniper rifle or something like that.

For now, I have no way to warn her. My gaze darts back and forth between them. She finally reaches the pile of stones. The bush is about thirty yards from her. The battle could begin in less than a second. I take a chance and leave my shelter. I make the sign meaning danger. When she turns around, she isn't looking at me, but at the bush. She crouches down and grabs a shotgun. A clear shot rings through the air, like a whip. The bush disappears, leaving behind materials, potions, first aid kits, accessories, and weapons. The biggest arsenal I've ever seen, scattered across the grass. From where I'm standing, it looks like the remains of a flea market after a free-for-all.

With a gesture, we agree to meet up by the loot. Like vultures, we swoop down on our prey's remains. Ella takes two seconds to build another shelter and we calmly sort through the various objects. However, there's so much stuff that we can't carry it all, forcing us to keep only what's necessary. While I'm debating between a first aid kit and blue potions, Ella signals for me to stop moving.

She seems concerned, and I quickly see why. An enemy, given away by the sound of his glider, shoots out of the sky, heading straight for us. She opens a hole in the roof, then closes it right away. The operation lasted less than one second, but that's all it took to recognize the Angel of Death's silhouette. Oh no! We're in a bad spot. A REALLY bad spot. I hardly have time to turn before she disappears, and the only sign she was there is a small opening at the back of our shelter. I hesitate to go outside, too. I could be more of a burden than any help. The first shots ring out. At the same time, the sound of construction echoes all around me. I'm listening to a concert of automatic weapons, interspersed with the thunderous explosions of pump-action shotguns. Suddenly, a dull sound ends the bizarre symphony.

A massive building fell, causing whoever was perched on top to fall to the ground violently.

I can't stay inside the shelter anymore. If Ella fell, I absolutely have to get her something to treat herself. I crawl through the hole in the wall. As I exit, I see different structures full of bullet holes. I circle my shelter and find myself nose to nose with the Angel of Death, squatting under a stone ramp. He's swallowing a blue potion. Upon seeing me, he immediately stops drinking and grabs his pump-action shotgun. In a panic, I turn back. The first round of bullets hits me in the back. The second tears up the shelter. I'm shaken, but my survival instincts urge me to hide again. I don't have to think about what I'm doing. Once inside, I start plugging up the opening I came in through. I know he's going to come after me.

While I repair the shelter, I hear footsteps combined with the sound of a gun being unloaded. In several seconds, chaos will rain down on me. Without hesitation, I create a second roof and slide under it. It's not guaranteed to save my life, but it will slow my enemy long enough for Ella to come help.

He attacks the shelter with his pickaxe! One wall crumbles. What's he doing? Strangely, instead of destroying it completely, the Angel of Death is replacing my wall with another. The clicking and pinging sounds give it away. He has just set a trap on the wall he built. Without the extra roof protecting me, I would already be a shish kebab on iron spikes.

My break is not long-lived. He attacks another wall with his pickaxe. He clearly knows that his trap didn't work and now he'll have to build a second one assuming the first one had a defect or something like that. Unfortunately, this time, he'll surely think to look inside first. He'll quickly see what's happening and then I won't have an emergency exit . . .

The second wall falls and, as predicted, he figures out my strategy. He begins attacking my roof with a pickaxe. I only have a second before my shelter crumbles. Appearing behind him, Ella unleashes a single shot directly into his head. He was so busy coming after me that he didn't see her coming. BOOM! The second shot sounds. The round of bullets enters a wall that the Angel of Death just built in a hurry to protect himself. Then Ella relentlessly unloads her magazine into the wall, which the man in black hurries to repair to protect himself from the bullets. When Ella reloads her two weapons, he creates a gap in the opposite wall. Then he escapes and closes the hole right when she penetrates my shelter.

It's awful! The trap goes off with a cold metallic noise when she passes by it. She narrowly jumps away and is seriously hurt, but she remains standing and full of rage. She empties another magazine to get rid of the danger. That done, she starts building another shelter. I leave my hiding spot and join her. We're reunited again in a small box. This time, though, it's made of iron, much sturdier than the others we built in the past.

While bandaging our wounds, our gazes cross. We know that several yards away, the monster is still there, bandaging himself, too, and unfortunately using the ceasefire to prepare a strategy. He has to solve the problem we've created for him: two against one. The sooner Ella returns to combat, the better our chances of eliminating him. She hugs me before creating a door, then sets out on the attack again, making a gesture telling me to stay hidden. I watch her close me in with a small twinge. Maybe I should break my promise to never touch a gun. Could I change my destiny with a gun in my hand?

Here we go again. The sound of constant shooting starts again. The building . . . The explosions . . . I feel fury growing inside me. That's when I hear the sound of the trampoline, that weird contraption capable of shooting you high enough into the air to deploy your glider. I know that Ella doesn't have one. Therefore it must belong to the Angel of Death. I have to take away his major advantage to destabilize him and ruin his plan of attack. I leave my hiding spot again. I see two new towers, each built by the two adversaries. The high-tech trampoline stands at the bottom of one of them. A well-thought-out location! It allows the attacker to fall from very high up without being hurt and to go right back up. His enemy, convinced she saw him descend, will look for him below, but be taken by surprise from above.

I run full-speed toward the machine. I'm shocked by another combatant's arrival. He joins the battle via a ramp he built in between the two towers. He is located directly above my head. I don't know who it is, but I can tell that he is very sure of himself. Each safe in their own tower, Ella and the Angel of Death stop shooting at each other to focus on the new person. He grabs a rocket launcher and shoots rockets to his left, then to his right. He's practically shooting at point-blank range. The explosions make the structures unstable.

Analyzing the new enemy's rhythm, Ella comes out of her shelter the moment he targets the Angel of Death. When he

turns to shoot at her, she is already close enough to him to build a wall between them. Before he can assess the situation, he shoots his weapon. The rocket explodes against the barrier, causing the man to disappear in a cloud of smoke. All his materials scatter along the remaining stairs, walls, and ramps.

His rocket launcher falls at my feet. I've barely noticed it before another battle has begun: the Angel of Death, taking advantage of Ella's attack on their mutual enemy, has improved his position and is now raining shots down on her from every destructive item in his arsenal. He knows that it's just the three of us and that I'm not a threat to him. She won't last long.

Taken by surprise, she can't retaliate, so she puts all of her energy into maintaining her shelter. On his end, between rounds, our enemy increases the pressure by building a walkway connecting the two towers. Little by little, he inches closer to her. In a few seconds, he will reach her. Our destruction seems inevitable. I take a deep breath and, with the accuracy and speed of an elite shooter, I pick up the rocket launcher, point it at the Angel of Death, and pull the trigger. The rocket shoots out toward the walkway. My finger still hovering over the trigger, my gaze settles on Ella. I hear another shot. NO! In my panic, I lower my weapon and, before realizing anything, the automatic weapon goes off and a second projectile flies out, blowing up the entire structure and sending Ella and the Angel of Death falling through the open sky.

Back live, on the set of *Battle for Domination*, the host gloats.

"How wild! It's outrageous! This is absolutely incredible! Since this show started, we've never seen anything like this! You still have a few minutes to vote and you could be the next one to participate in the *Battle for Domination*! After a short break, we'll be back in the participants' room to hear what today's winner decides!"

18

THE EXIT IS THIS WAY!

"Are you excited?"

The audience, with a single voice, responds in chorus, "Yeeessss!"

"I can't hear you. ARE YOU EXCITED?"

"YEEESSS!"

The host of *Battle for Domination* knows that the show has hit its peak audience during this final battle. It's the perfect time to start the advertisements. The giant screen, looming above the stage, displays them all: an optometrist selling his new line of eyeglasses, number one on the market. A hardware store claims to be ranked number one because of the quality of its construction materials. Candy to reward children who worked hard all day . . .

The sound is muted in the stadium so that the host can keep the audience's excitement high. When the live feed starts back up, it has to look like a massive party. Everyone in front of their television, computer, tablet, and phone, has to be dying to participate. The countdown begins in the master of ceremony's ear. In ten seconds, he will pump up his audience again.

"Make some NOISE!"

He moves to the front of the stage and, with one hand next to his ear, he repeats, "I can't hear you! MAKE SOME NOISE!"

Broadcasting live, the host continues his one-man-show while crossing the length of the stage. He wants the entire stadium participating.

"*BATTLE FOR?*"

"*DOMINATION!*"

After the fifth time, he applauds his audience.

"You're amazing!"

He runs up to a camera, gives it a wink, then speaks directly to it: "And you, too, you're fantastic! I hear you shouting and clapping at home. I love it! What a crazy night! Now, we're ready to go live to the participants' room and finally hear what today's winner has decided."

Suddenly, someone speaks to him in his earpiece. He appears a little thrown off, then gathers himself.

"But, before that, let's watch the outcome of this historic battle one more time."

The giant screen displays a suspenseful montage of the titanic battle that pitted Ella and Paul against the Angel of Death. The sequence plays over loud music and is full of slow-motion scenes, replays, and special effects . . . Fascinated by these images, the audience shouts with joy every time a shot hits its target and claps after each explosion.

The host has gone backstage. He's standing with Mark, the game's creator and producer. Their conversation seems very animated, even tense.

. . .

A little earlier, in the massive control room of the medical complex, a team of technicians and doctors is on high alert. They check the contestants and make sure their operations function correctly. One of the managers, his eyes glued to his computer screen, is startled. A window just opened with an especially loud "thwack." With an annoyed tone, he shouts, "Hey, guys! Be careful when you change the volume on the compu . . ."

To establish his authority, he pauses a moment. Then he goes on in a slightly more relaxed tone, "OK, we're set. We have our winner for the day. Prepare subject 45 for an impending exit, please."

He has barely finished speaking when the lights start flickering eerily.

"What's happening?"

At the other end of the room, someone speaks up,

"The converters and generator have kicked in. Clearly, there's a problem with the energy supply."

A wave of panic spreads over the room. Across multiple screens, error messages stack up. At various work stations, the operators report the information out loud. They sound discouraging.

He has to get out

"Unable to stabilize the flow! We're experiencing blackouts."

"The same for the computers; the network is extremely unstable!"

"The game has crashed, guys! The system is doing its best to recover. It doesn't look good!"

Glued to his phone, the manager approaches the control panel that handles the video stream on television.

"We have a severe blackout here! I couldn't warn Mark. If you can find him, tell him we're in real trouble here. Nothing can be done. For now, we can't process the contestant's exit. I have to go. I'll keep you updated!"

The head operator hangs up. In the enormous room where hundreds of screens display the images coming from *Battle for Domination*, everything is tense. The manager decides to address his team.

"Guys, listen up! We can't count on the medical center for now. They're having serious technical problems. That means the player can't be taken out until we get new orders. Assemble replays, player profiles, best of's, anything Mark says to play . . . I want everything ready yesterday! Is that clear, everyone?"

Just as he finishes speaking, his phone rings. It's Mark checking in because he can't get ahold of anyone on set. He is receiving the alerts from the medical center on his phone, as well as a dozen other messages. Annoyed, he won't stop shouting. The manager tries everything to calm him down.

"Mark. Listen to me, Mark! I talked to the center a few minutes ago. An exit's impossible for now. They're totally lost over there. We don't know how long it will be before it's fixed.

The game has crashed. The servers will reboot when they're ready, but no one knows what that means for the players."

Despite the manager's serious, robust voice, Mark continues to scream, and the shouts on the other end of the phone echo through the room. Fortunately for him, the other man was careful to not hold the phone near his ear.

"Mark! Come on, listen to me! We have everything ready: the bios, best of's, and recaps. We have to fill less than ten minutes of live coverage; that's not much."

After more shouting, the conversation ends. The manager hangs up.

. . .

I'm on Big Island. Not in an unknown place, but on the cliff with the isolated house, the one with the ice cream truck. We're all here and, strangely, we've all regained our voices! The situation has surprised all the participants. I'm completely lost, and clearly I'm not the only one. What exactly happened? My last memory is of that big battle. I only remember an enormous flash. Then . . . I suddenly found myself here, surrounded by these people. Incredible! I quickly look around the area and notice there are no weapons here, not even a pickaxe. No one can attack each other or destroy anything. Plus, the powerful magnetic field preventing us from leaving the islands has now shrunk to contain this small area. Ah! Ah! Ah! Now we're all stuck here. I have to find Ella as soon as possible.

I'm very thankful that we're not fighting anymore, but the symphony of voices around me is thrilling, too. Everyone is asking questions. Everyone has an idea about our status.

"What's happening?"

"Is the game over?"

"Are we all leaving?"

While I wander through the crowd, I notice that the questions quickly develop into basic, friendly conversations. The players are getting to know and like each other. It's amazing.

Music suddenly fills our ears, as if out of nowhere. Some people start dancing. The farther I go through the crowd, the more my discoveries surprise me. Vending machines spread all over the area are giving away drinks for free. People who love ice cream are gathered around the truck, full and happy. It seems this site is now completely dedicated to partying. About a hundred people are talking, laughing, and doing strange dances.

I'm happy. I'm so happy to be able to say, "pardon me," "I'm sorry," and "excuse me." Every word out of my mouth leaves a sweet taste on my tongue. It feels great to be able to communicate! I would love to enjoy this with Ella.

"Paul?"

The sound startles me, then I turn around to see her there, less than three feet away. She holds an ice cream cone in each hand. I leap with joy and let out a loud, high-pitched squeal. Suddenly embarrassed, I don't dare look her in the eyes. I try to get ahold of myself by focusing on the ice cream in her hands. At first glance, I'd guess strawberry on the right, chocolate on the left. She extends her right hand to me.

"I brought you an ice cream cone. I just know you're the kind of guy who likes strawberry!"

Wrong! My favorite flavor is chocolate. But for her, I'll become a "strawberry guy" without a second thought.

"How'd you guess? And I bet you're a chocolate girl!"

"Bingo! We don't know each other well, but I'm sure we'll get along great . . ."

"Yep!"

So here we are, celebrating our reunion without a word, just enjoying our ice cream.

I feel obligated to break the silence.

"It's crazy what just happened."

"Yup, pretty surprising. Let's enjoy it. Before things go back to the way they were. Come with me . . ."

She takes my arm and leads me to the wooden dock that overlooks the cliff edge. We sit next to each other, our feet dangling out in the open. Without planning it, we start spinning them in the air, like pedaling a bicycle. Big Island stretches out before us. The landscape seems more beautiful than ever.

"It's a pretty wonderful place after all, isn't it?"

"Thanks, Paul. Thanks for everything you did for me earlier. You didn't have to pick up that gun to help me. But you did it anyway. I can't imagine how difficult that was for you to go back on your promise. You can't imagine how much that meant to me . . ."

I want to respond, but I can't. My throat is tight. I try to hold my tears back. After a couple of forced breaths, I'm ready. In a wavering voice, I say, "I didn't think about it. The thought of you getting hurt . . . I don't know . . . Well . . . That's it."

In response, she takes my hand and gently leans her head on my shoulder. My heart feels like it's going to explode. I don't know how long this will last. I don't even know if it's real. What I do know is that, at this exact moment, I've never been happier. In turn, I lightly lean my head against hers.

How long did we stay like that together? I can't say . . . I could have stayed next to her my entire life . . .

I start dreaming of the trips we'd go on, the movies and TV shows we'd watch together.

Wonderful thoughts start dancing wildly through my head, giving me a dizzy feeling that abruptly yanks me out of my daydreams. I flinch and try to find something to grab onto to regain my balance. Then I hear a strange buzzing. Lifting my head, I notice a small drone circling above us. It finally floats in place and emits a beam of light. It increases in intensity, then engulfs my entire body. With a flash of light, I feel myself being carried away. I feel myself disappear.

In the next second, I can't move or even talk. My gaze sweeps over the area. Clearly, I'm wearing some kind of scuba diving mask. Before my eyes, a screen finally lights up and a message starts playing. I find it extremely difficult to make out what it says. I feel sick. My nose itches and my face tingles all over. The text, which plays over and over, is quite simple:

"WELL DONE! YOU ARE THE WINNER OF *BATTLE FOR DOMINATION!*"

I find it difficult to believe at first, but little by little, I start to understand the meaning of the statement. That's it! I'm going to be able to get out of here! The whole ordeal is finally over. Then another message appears, giving me two options: return to Small Island or leave forever. To make me choice: blinking my eyes once means I stay, blinking twice means I leave.

Freedom! I'm about to blink, but then I reconsider. What lies outside for me? What will I be able to do? Become a movie star? Those are all concerns that suddenly move to the back of my mind, as Ella now fills my thoughts. I see her running next to me on our adventures. I remember her head resting gently on my shoulder, like a butterfly. I have plenty of time to become an actor later, but now, at this moment, my place is next to her. Nowhere else. I'll go back!

I close my eyes tight to make sure my choice registers. One clear blink. Warmth washes over me. My facial muscles contract and this itchy feeling in my nose makes me sneeze. I try to hold it in so I don't splatter snot across the glass of my diving mask. Whew, I must be as red as a tomato, but at least I avoided the worst: nothing came out of me. A new message appears,

"YOU HAVE CHOSEN TO LEAVE! CONGRATS!"

No! I did not! I want to stay! Wrapped up tight like a sausage, I can't move. The message plays over and over, congratulating me on my alleged choice. It makes me crazy. A whistle, like that of a tea kettle, sounds. A sort of fog is injected into my diving mask.

I'm annoyed, but I notice that the fog floating around me calms me down.

Less than one minute later, the screen and my entire diving mask have disappeared. I realize that I'm standing in an immaculate white room. At the back, I notice about ten people. They're wearing full bodysuits with artificial breathing systems. I feel like I'm in a science fiction movie.

"Paul? Can you hear me? You're live on our show, *Battle for Domination*! Paul, the whole world is watching you!"

The voice speaking to me comes from a different screen located approximately one yard away from me. On it, I see a man in the middle of an enormous stage. In a square on the screen, I recognize myself, too. My head sticks out of the diving suit I'm still wearing. I realize that I'm on a video conference call. I try to answer and stammer out a very unconvincing "Hello."

"Paul! Congratulations! You're the first person in the world to leave the game!"

I hear applause and cheers behind the man's voice.

"Why did you choose to leave? It's your first victory. It's just the beginning . . . Don't you want to be more famous and win more money?"

"I . . . I made a mistake . . ."

"Excuse me? What did you say, Paul?"

"I don't want to leave . . . I made a mistake. I want to go back to the game."

"Ladies and gentlemen, something incredible is happening! Paul, did we hear you correctly? You want to return to the chaos of *Battle for Domination*?"

"Yes."

"Great! That's very brave! That's the *Battle for Domination* spirit! Why did you change your mind?"

Ella's face haunts me. I want to see her, meet her again. I belong next to her.

"Paul? Are you OK? Why do you want to stay?"

I think for a long time. Then I find a reply that I think sounds really cool. I announce, "It's my secret . . . And you haven't seen anything yet! You haven't heard the last from me!"

A round of applause.

"I think you just won some more fans, Paul."

The presenter then suddenly leaves the camera's view, showing me the enormous crowd going wild.

"You've made your choice, Paul! Don't disappoint us. We're counting on YOU!"

Look for these books!